who ordered a
MEDIUM
AN UNFORTUNATE SPELLS NOVELLA

Sometimes you find love in unexpected place.

Jennifer Laslie

JENNIFER LASLIE

OTHER BOOKS BY JENNIFER LASLIE

The Unfortunate Spells Series

Who Ordered a Medium (Novella)

When to Spell Disaster (#1)

When to Scry Wolf (#2)

What the Hex Happened (#3)

Why Didn't You Ward Me (#4)

Where Are My Solsticers (#5)

The Thicker Than Blood Series

Marked for Death (#1)

Untreatable

Mermaid Adrift

Sordid Depths

Azure Embers

Forbidden Throne

Solstice Flames - Jingle Spells Anthology

Rae of Hope - Twisted Fairy Tales Anthology

Exiled - A Midsummer Night's Sidhe Anthology

I

"We're all out of tequila," Lora howled over the pop music blaring through the speakers. The purple tips of her blonde hair swished behind her as she turned to face the rest of us. "Who drank all the tequila?" She slammed the bottle onto Valerie's white marble island, and a small crack split up the side of the bottle and veined out.

For over three hours, my bachelorette party had been going strong. Somehow, Valerie had talked Helen and Lora into having it at her house.

Having the party at Valerie's home sorta made sense, considering her house boasted an in-ground pool, a theater room, and a basement with a pool table. The therapist life treated her well.

Valerie, tenuous friend but expert drinker, held her empty shot glass close to her chest. She sucked in a breath through her teeth. "This should be a crime." She set the glass down and snatched up a bottle of rum with the flourish only a well-libated individual could accomplish. "No worries, there's plenty of rum! Here, I'll pour you another shot, Josie."

I reluctantly slid my shot glass over to Valerie. The party wasn't going as planned. The balloons hadn't stayed in the air in a perfect arch. Instead, they lay on the grass, looking like a sick pink-and-purple anaconda. The pool heater had broken, leaving the water too frigid to wade in at night, let alone swim. On top of all that, the alcohol appeared to be dwindling before my eyes.

Our game of Pin the Penis on the Groom had ended when Lora pinned one on Helen's face, repeatedly. Somehow, the injury required more than one Band-Aid. I still wasn't sure how many times Lora had stabbed Helen with the pin. The blood prevented us from counting each little hole. We should have used tape instead of a thumbtack.

Who knew a face wound could bleed so much? I only hoped the blood I'd accidentally gotten in my blonde hair, when I'd scratched an itch on my cheek, would come out in the shower.

"Bottoms up!" Helen squealed as she downed another bout of liquid courage, and the others followed suit.

I tipped mine back and slammed the glass down seconds after the others. The rum burned its way down my throat to join the tequila.

"Maybe we should've gone out," I nonchalantly squeezed into the conversation. Maybe they'd be too drunk to realize I wasn't having as much fun as them.

"What? No!" Valerie shook her head overdramatically. "The better question is... are you sure you want to marry Doug?"

2

Valerie had definitely gone a *tad* over her limit, and by a tad, I really meant way too much. She always gloated about how well she could hold her liquor. She was a Houdini at making the liquor disappear, but a question like that, two days before my wedding, was uncalled for.

"How could you ask me that?" I sent a heated glare Valerie's way, wondering if her question was the alcohol talking, or if she truly wanted an answer.

Before Valerie could reply, Helen wiggled up next to me, a conspiratorial gleam in her eyes. "We've got a surprise for you, Josie," she sing-songed. "Just wait!" She patted my shoulder, and then whispered in Lora's ear, whose eyes lit up moments later.

My *Adios Motherfucker* beckoned. I took a sip through the tip of my penis-shaped straw, filing Valerie's question into the far recesses of my mind.

The doorbell chimed, though I could barely hear it over the music and chatter.

Valerie busied herself with pouring more shots. "Hey, Josie. You think you can get that?"

"Um, yeah. Sure." I adjusted my *Bride To Be* sash and went to answer the door.

The door swung inward, revealing a strikingly handsome man in a slate-gray button up shirt and tight-fitting jeans. The sides of his hair were buzzed close to his head, but the top hung down, sweeping into his baby blues.

The man at the door grimaced. "Sorry. The day job ran over." He exuded sexuality, and the frown marring his face only made him look more appetizing.

I raked my gaze down him, drinking him in. I wondered if

he had a *straw* I could drink from, but then mentally smacked myself. My wedding was in two days.

Doug. I was marrying Doug. That didn't mean I couldn't live it up before then. Right?

"Valerie?" The man cleared his throat, and I snapped out of my daze.

I shook my head. "I'm Josie."

Suddenly, Ginuwine's *Pony* started up behind me over the sound system.

Oh, Lord. They'd ordered a stripper. No one played a song like that unless they were stripping.

"Josie," he purred as he pushed his way past me, brushing a hand along my arm.

I swallowed painfully, trying to wet my mouth and throat.

The music took over his body, his hips swaying to a deep bass vibrating the hardwood floor. He kicked off his shoes and slid easily across the floor in his socked feet.

My three best friends ran out from behind the kitchen island, stumbling over each other.

"No! He's mine!" Lora yelled, snagging Helen by the shirt. Lora's efforts earned her and Helen a place on the floor while Valerie skirted around them, barely managing to keep herself upright.

When I turned back to the stripper, his jeans were already in a heap on the floor.

He winked at me and lip synched to the music, *Come and jump on it!* His hands framed the area where his extremely small undies bulged.

The drunken gears in my head started turning,

wondering if my friends had ordered a stripper or a prostitute. Prostitutes were still illegal, right?

My *Adios Motherfucker* appeared in my hand. Valerie's sly smile greeted me out of the corner of my eye. "I thought you might need a little more liquid courage."

"Oh!" Something hit the back of my knees, and I dropped down into one of the cushioned dining room chairs. My hand automatically shot out to try to stabilize the drink in my hand. The liquid inside sloshed back and forth like an angry sea... with a penis straw floating in it.

I giggle-snorted. The shots of tequila the girls had foisted on me were warming my blood and dulling my judgement.

From my new vantage point, the stripper's chiseled abs were eye level as he sauntered near. He peeled off the sleeves of his shirt. The garment flew through the air to land beside his jeans, leaving him in only the super-tight undies.

If only Doug didn't have a dad bod, but... But I loved his dad bod. My alcohol addled brain didn't realize I shouldn't compare my fiancé to a stripper. I immediately felt guilty for having those thoughts.

His hands grabbed my knees roughly and spread my legs wide. With practiced precision, he dipped his head between my legs and rose up slowly, his labored breath fanning across my face.

"No frowning," he spoke against the shell of my ear.

Goosebumps rose along my arms and legs, traveling at a rapid pace, while heat pooled down low. I bit my lip to keep from moaning and shook my head. "No, no more frowning."

He lifted my chin and gave me a megawatt smile. "That's my girl."

His girl?

I started to frown, confused, but he pressed a finger to my lips. "Nope."

He spun on his heels, dropped down to his knees, and leaned back to let his arms support him. Those hips rolled and thrust in my direction with vigor.

I bet he was amazing in bed.

Eep! I threw a hand over my mouth, but soon realized I'd only thought it in my head. *No, no no no.* There would be no thoughts of having sex with the stripper tonight.

Maybe I could just touch him. My fingers itched to reach out and explore the hard planes of his sweat-slickened chest.

Helen crawled over to him on all fours as he stood. "Can I lick you?"

He bowed and slid away from her with a wink as the song ended. The sound system went back to the regular playlist, and Mr. Handsome started dressing himself.

Lora gasped. "Why are you getting dressed?"

I looked up to find Valerie sneaking back to the kitchen.

"Valerie?" Helen wobbled precariously as she tried to stand up, pointing angrily at the stripper. "Why is he getting dressed?"

As he buttoned up his shirt, he stepped over to whisper in my ear. "I apologize. Your friend only paid for one song."

The smell of incense and smoke rolled off him, something I hadn't noticed when he was pressed between my legs. The scent wasn't manly, but somehow still called to something within me. I felt this draw, and I wondered if he felt it, too.

I leaned into him to get a better whiff.

"Josie?" He didn't move. The corner of his lip twitched. "Did you just sniff me?" Some other emotion replaced his amusement, but I couldn't place it. Not in my current inebriated state.

"I...I think I did." I quickly leaned back and plastered myself against the chair. "I'm so sorry. I don't know what's come over me. It must be the alcohol."

He nodded and, straightened, sporting a tight-lipped smile. "Congratulations on your upcoming nuptials."

My cheeks burned. I'd just sniffed a stranger and here he stood reminding me I was getting married soon.

"Thank you." I turned away to hide my shame and found Helen and Lora digging through their purses. Valerie had disappeared to God knows where.

As I turned back, the front door clicked shut.

"I found it!" Lora screamed in triumph. She threw her purse on the counter and unzipped her wallet. She glanced up from her task long enough to catch my look of shock.

"Where'd he go?" Fishing a wad of cash from her wallet, Lora's eyes surveyed the living room. "I need to pay for another... song." She dropped her arms to her side, and the money scattered around her on the floor.

"He's gone, Lora." Pressing the tip of my penis straw to my lips, I sucked down the rest of my drink. Tonight had been fun. I'd spent time with my friends, got a surprise lap dance, and watched Lora and Helen makes fools of themselves as they tried to find buried treasure in their purses for the stripper.

A vibration erupted from my pocket, overpowering my

dulled senses. I set my drink on the ground before I spilled it and pulled out my phone.

A message from Doug: *When will you be home?*

I knew he was only worried about me. Did I tell him we were going to Valerie's house for the party? I couldn't remember. Perhaps he thought I was out on the town.

I sent a quick text back to Doug, pulled up the Uber app to order a ride, and then put my phone back in my pocket. "Guys, I'm going to head home." Helen and Lora groaned from the window. Both had the blinds cracked and were peering out at the street.

"What are you all doing?" I pushed the chair under the dining room table and grabbed my purse. The two hadn't answered me. "Lora? Helen?"

"What?" Lora said without turning around.

Helen jumped out of her skin when I laid a hand on her shoulder. "Oh!"

"I'm heading home. My ride should be here soon."

"He really is gone," Lora whined.

A loud crash came from the kitchen. We all turned to find Valerie slumped on a stool with her head on the counter. Beside her feet, a rum bottle had hit the tile and shattered into tiny pieces.

"Valerie, don't move!" I said.

Outside, a car horn beckoned. Damnit. My ride was here.

"Go on," Helen coaxed. "We'll clean this mess up. I've gotta get home soon anyways. Roy probably hasn't even put the kids to bed yet."

"You sure?"

As Helen sighed and tugged Lora toward the kitchen, the

latter waved me away. "Yes, go. We've got this. Tonight was for you to have fun, not clean up after Valerie."

"Hey, I represent that," Valerie slurred from her resting place on the island.

"Exactly." Lora rolled her eyes.

I raced over and hugged Lora and Helen, thanking them for taking care of the mess, and slipped out the door.

Once home, I found Doug waiting for me on the couch, snoring. An impressive pile of broken down boxes lay on one side of the living room. He'd definitely gotten a lot of unpacking done while I was out. We'd just bought and moved into the Victorian-style house with a wraparound porch. The structure stood strong, but needed a few updates.

Doug looked so peaceful sprawled out on the couch with his arm thrown over his eyes, I almost didn't want to wake him.

Before I could touch his shoulder, his arm shifted and eyes opened halfway. "Josie?"

"Yeah?" I whispered. I didn't know why I whispered. We were the only two in the house.

"Did you have fun?" His question came out mumbled, sleep trying to pull him back under.

I smiled. "I did. We had the party at Valerie's house and..." I almost slipped and told him about the stripper. Doug may not have minded, but I knew he'd been concerned about what all my bachelorette party would include. One song was barely enough to worry about.

"And?" He asked groggily.

"And it was nice. We had some drinks, listened to music, and played a few games."

"That *is* nice."

Grabbing his hands, I pulled him into a sitting position. "Come on, honey. Let's get you to bed."

I decided I'd not mention the stripper tonight. Doug's best friends were taking him out tomorrow, and Jacob and Mike were even rowdier than my friends. I'd bet money his friends would do more damage than mine.

2

Outside, lightning split the sky in half. I flicked the blinds closed and turned to Doug. "Maybe you should stay home." I nearly jumped into his arms as a peal of thunder followed closely behind it. "Jesus!"

Doug waved my concern away. "I'll be fine. The radar shows it's almost over. You got to go out last night. Now, it's my turn." He shrugged on his jacket and kissed me goodbye. "Don't stay up."

"You know I will." I leaned close and rubbed a hand over his shaved head.

"I know." He grinned. "Saturday will start our forever together. This is only one night."

I threw my arms around him and hugged him tight, my face smashed into the crook of his neck. "Be safe," I mumbled against his skin.

He squeezed back and then released me. "Always."

Doug walked out and closed the storm door before the wind could grab hold. I watched him through the glass as he ran to his car, his arms thrown over his head like they could protect him from the rain.

Inside his car, he gave me a wave, then pulled away from the curb.

I returned the wave and blew him a kiss.

Another bolt of lightning spooked me. I slammed the door, threw the lock in place, and retreated a safe distance. Like the lightning could open up the door and get me.

Growing up in Oklahoma gave me every right to be afraid of storms. My parents moved us down to Austin when I was twelve, but by that time, the fear of storms had been ingrained in me as well as my own fingerprints.

I shook off the feeling of impending doom. Time to unpack a few more boxes to help pass the time while Doug was away. No telling how long he'd be out with his friends. Probably later than I was last night.

Bang! Clap!

The noise caught me off guard. I cringed and crept to the window, lifting the blinds to look outside. *God, I hate storms.* The lightning didn't bother me so much. When the thunder followed, that was the issue. I hated the loud noise.

The clatter outside wasn't thunder, though.

Bang! Snap!

Maybe one of the gutters had fallen or a branch was hitting the side of the house. I hoped one of the trees next to the house hadn't fallen over with all the wind gusts.

Unease settled deep in my stomach. Maybe I should wait for Doug to get home. But what if it was something I could easily repair? I needed to know what damage there was outside and to see if I could minimize it.

In the hall closet, I found my raincoat, and took a steadying breath as I put it on. The storm was only wind and rain.

Wind and rain, Josie. Wind and rain.

The thunder rumbled farther away and the lightning was small and distant. Neither could hurt me.

I could do this.

The locks had been replaced before we moved in and the deadbolt slid with ease. I slowly opened the door. The storm door shuddered at the force of the wind, rattling in its frame.

It's just a little wind I told myself.

I weighed too much to blow away, thank goodness. Hips don't lie.

My phone buzzed in my pocket. I realized I hadn't taken it off vibrate from last night when I went to bed. I had a couple texts from Valerie apologizing about the stripper.

Helen had texted me early this morning to make sure I'd made it home okay and that my Uber driver hadn't abducted me and sold me to a sex trafficking ring. Frantic texts continued, followed by apologies if she'd woken me up at any point.

I couldn't help but shake my head at the two of them. Leisurely scrolling through my texts and emails, I did my best to get caught up from the past couple days. How did one person get that many emails?

When I finally finished, I decided to text Valerie back to accept her apology, but my phone started ringing.

Bang!

"Eep!" I jumped and ran to the couch to answer the phone without looking to see who it was. "Hello?"

"Hey, sexy," Doug slurred over the music blaring in the background. "I sure do miss you. You're still at home right?"

"Doug?" The voice almost didn't sound like him. "Are you drunk?"

The music died down to a hum. He must have walked somewhere quieter. Doug stayed silent for a while.

"Doug? Are you there?"

"Josie? Oh, hey. I didn't know you'd called me." He laughed. "W-what are you wearing?"

"Where are you?" Maybe Jacob and Mike had taken him to one of the clubs downtown.

The phone scraped against something. "Oh, me? I'm at Club Zee."

Club Zee? What was he doing at a strip club downtown in the seedier part of the city? How could his friends have thought going there would be a good idea?

Deep breath. I'd had a hot stripper give me a lap dance last night, and Doug didn't even know about it. I didn't have any room to throw stones in this glass house we'd constructed. These parties were our last nights of freedom before marriage. I'd let it slide.

"Doug, I've gotta go." I pressed the phone between my shoulder and ear as I stood from the couch. Buttoning my raincoat, I headed back toward the door. "I need to go outside and check on something. I love you."

"Love y—" the line went dead before he could even finish saying *you.*

At least he was having fun.

Clap! B-bang!

This house wasn't going to fix itself. Shoving my phone

in my back pocket, I braced myself against the storm door and pushed it open against the wind. When I slipped past, it whipped shut with a crash of metal against wood.

I hugged my arms around my midsection as my hair whipped around my head. Everything on the porch looked like it was in one piece. Around the side of the house, both trees stood strong against the onslaught of the storm.

Leaves swirled around the yard. Something wet smacked me in the face, half of the mysterious substance going in my mouth when I opened it to yelp. I grabbed at it and threw it off of me, my heart pounding.

A leaf. It was just a leaf. Not a bug. Not a serial killer.

Right hand clutched to my chest, I took a moment to catch my breath.

Bang! The noise came from right beside me.

I shrieked and jerked to look toward the clamor. My foot slipped, and I stumbled back into the house.

Beside me, the window shutter rattled against the house. The wind picked up and the slatted wood flew to the left, smacked into the window frame, and then whipped back against the house.

Sleep would be hard won if this continued through the night. I needed to at least nail it down until Doug could either fix or replace the offending object.

All of his tools were in the detached garage.

I ran inside and grabbed my keys. When I left the safety of the porch, I did my best to dodge the raindrops. I shoved the key into the lock of the side door and hurried inside.

The lightbulb buzzed and winked before finally staying on. There wasn't much in the garage, but I remembered him carrying a large, red toolbox in here. Surely I'd find a hammer in there, maybe a couple nails.

I spotted a flash of red behind a few boxes and weaved my way over there. The toolbox itself and the latches were rusted. I had to fight with the latch on the left to get it to unlock. *Luck be a lady tonight.* Inside the box, I found a hammer. And underneath the top tray, I found a box of nails long enough to secure the shutter.

I pocketed four nails and gripped the hammer tight.

With the garage locked up, I raced back to the porch.

My phone rang once again. I pulled it out of my pocket and saw Doug's name flash across the screen.

Wiping a wet finger across the screen, I answered. "Doug?"

"Hey, hey, hey!" Doug shouted into the phone. In the background, *Pour Some Sugar on Me* blared.

"Doug, just call me when you leave the club. Stop drunk calling me, and for God's sakes, get an Uber tonight." I hung up before he could say anything else.

The shutter proved easy to wrangle. I pushed it against the house and hammered in all four nails down the edge of it.

Stepping back, I surveyed my work. The shutter should hold for the night. Doug could fix it later after he'd gotten over his hangover. He was in for a world of hurt from the sound of it.

Back inside, I took the steps two at a time, and got to business in our bedroom. Our room and bathroom took up the whole front of the upstairs. The windows didn't have curtains yet, only blinds. Every little lightning flash had my nerves on edge.

I'd thought Doug had said the storm was almost over. The wind still howled, causing the bones of the house to creak and groan. Getting used to the noises of an old house would take some time.

Tackling the bathroom first, I managed to get most of the boxes unpacked and the towels stacked neatly in the hall closet. A shower would feel like heaven tonight before bed.

Hands on hips, I stared at the obstacle course of scattered boxes around my bedroom.

Opening the first box I came upon, I found some of Doug's books. The shelf in our bedroom already lacked the space to put them all on display. I turned several of them sideways and stacked them up to fit more in there.

The second box I opened held clothes at the bottom. Hangers were tangled in a mass on top of them. Who packed this box? This was going to take forever.

Untangling the mass one by one, I put the hangers in the walk-in closet. I bit the inside of my lip as I caught sight of the opaque zip-up bag in the back.

My wedding dress. I couldn't wait to wear it Saturday and become Mrs. Branton. I wanted nothing to do with the Smallwood name. Not where my father was concerned.

Once again, my phone went off in my pocket. I swore under my breath while I yanked it out of my jeans. There was no way Doug could be on his way home. The hour was still young. If he was drunk dialing me again, he was in trouble.

"Damnit, Doug. You need to stop drunk dialing me and—"

"Ma'am," a soft masculine voice interrupted. "This is officer Javier Gomez with the APD. Is this Josie Branton?"

"Uh, yeah." My mind reeled. "I mean yes, this is she, but it's Smallwood. Josie Smallwood. I won't be a Branton until Saturday."

He cleared his throat. "My apologies, but your fiancé's been in an accident."

3

"What?" I held my breath.

"We tried to go by your house, but no one was home." He took a breath. "The house actually looked vacant, but we found your name in Doug's contact list with I-C-E next to it."

In Case of Emergency. We'd put each other in our phones like that. He'd even changed my last name to Branton in his phone since we'd been engaged.

"Look, if Doug got into some kind of fender bender, please just bring him home. And you probably used the old address from his license. We just moved." All these crazy scenarios kept playing on repeat in my head. I didn't even care if they had to tow the car. "You don't need to put him in the drunk tank. I can look after him until he sobers up." I'd never let him live this down. My bachelorette party hadn't gotten near as crazy as his.

"I'm afraid I won't be able to do that." Regret laced his words. "Is there anyone I can call to come get you?"

Oh no. What kind of trouble had Doug got himself into? If he had gotten himself locked up and couldn't make the wedding, so help me God… I couldn't afford to bail him out. Maybe Valerie could, but I didn't have that kind of cash.

"What did Doug do?"

"We can talk about that in a moment." The officer sighed, his patience clearly wearing thin. "Now, do you have someone who can come get you?"

"Officer Gomez, with all due respect, tell me what the fuck my soon-to-be-husband got himself into." I needed to mentally prepare and to possibly make a few phone calls.

"Ma'am, we found his car wrapped around a telephone pole. Paramedics arrived on scene, and he was rushed to the hospital."

"What?" The cop's earlier words came back to me. *I'm afraid we won't be able to do that.* What I originally thought was regret had been sympathy, but that wasn't right. People got into car accidents all the time and were fine. Some walked away without a scratch. Maybe it wasn't that bad, and Doug was only being sent to the hospital as a precautionary thing.

The officer cleared his throat. "I'm so sorry, ma'am, but it doesn't look good."

Shit. Okay, so his trip to the hospital wasn't for precautionary measures.

"They can still fix him, right?" My throat closed up, tears threatening to lay siege to my cheeks. The paramedics just needed to keep trying. I dashed down the stairs with the phone pressed to my ear. Snatching my purse and keys, I ran to the door.

"They're going to try." Hushed tones carried faintly through the line, like he was speaking with another officer. "Ma'am, just stay right there. Let me call someone to come get you."

"To hell with that. I don't have time to wait for a friend. What hospital did they take him to?" I squeezed my hand into a fist, the edges of the keys digging painfully into my palm. The pain helped keep me grounded.

The officer hesitated. His silence stretched out into agonizing seconds. Finally, he told me the hospital. "But... please be careful," he added. "The roads are still slick, and we're under a wind advisory until four in the morning. If you have a friend that can drive you, I'd advise you call them."

"Thank you, officer." I hung up before he could protest against me driving again.

MY FORD FOCUS made it to the hospital in record time without me breaking any traffic laws. Barely. Maybe. Okay, I broke a couple, but no one was around, so it didn't count.

I found a spot out in *Pluto Section Z* of the parking lot and raced to the emergency room doors with the wind whipping my hair into knots. I had to have looked like a drunken racoon, what with the running makeup from crying and my disheveled state due to the weather.

I ran past a waiting room full of people and skidded to a halt at the counter. Trying to catch my breath, I did my best not to ramble between labored huffs. I seriously needed to

JENNIFER LASLIE

work out more. "I'm looking for Doug Branton. Where can I find him?"

The frazzled girl behind the counter still managed to offer me a kind smile. She tucked an errant strand of hair that had fallen from her clip behind her ear. "Are you friend or family?" she asked calmly.

"Family," I blurted out. "I'm his wife. I was told he'd been in a car accident and brought to this hospital. Please... tell me he's okay!" My hand gripped the strap of my purse, trying to refrain from chucking something at her head to get her to talk faster.

"What was his name again?"

I growled in frustration. "Doug Branton."

The girl's fingers took their time typing in each letter of Doug's name.

"He's..." She looked over my shoulder into the large waiting room, then shook her head. She walked around from the counter, and with a hand on my back, guided me down the hall away from prying eyes. "Please have a seat. Your husband is currently in surgery. I'll page one of the doctors to come speak with you."

"Surgery?" Tears welled to the surface.

She merely nodded and helped me into a chair. "Someone will be out shortly."

The waiting grated on each and every nerve ending in my body, until every muscle hurt from clenching in anticipation. Would he be able to survive the surgery? What were they working on? Would he even be able to have a normal life afterwards? I had so many questions and zero answers.

26

I called Lora and wailed at her through the phone. It was a wonder she understood a word I said.

"Josie, breathe. I'm sure he'll be fine. Doug is too much of an... he's too stubborn to die on you."

A hiccup escaped me and made me break down into tears once again. Doug loved my hiccups. He'd mimic the sound whenever I'd get them. We both usually ended up in tears of laughter.

The tears streaming down my face were not followed by laughter this time.

"I need him to be okay," I said through sobs. "He's supposed to be my forever, remember?"

The receptionist ushered an older woman into the small waiting room with me, destroying my solitude. I pressed my lips closer to the phone and whispered, "What if we can't get married on Saturday?"

"Then you can push it back and get married another day." Lora sniffed, then let out a cough. "Listen, you hang tight, and I'll be right there to wait with you."

"No, no." I stood from the hard plastic chair and walked out of earshot from the room's other occupant. "I'll be fine."

No one was ever *fine* when they said they were or would be. And I was not the exception to the rule. My heart ached along with my over-tensed muscles.

"I'm sure you will, but just to be safe..." Lora trailed off. "See you soon."

I walked back to my chair and sank down into a puddle of anxiety mixed with a helping of grief. The receptionist had said someone would be out shortly to talk with me. How much longer could I wait before I had a meltdown? Ten more minutes? Twenty?

The second hand on the wall clock ticked by at a snail's pace. None of the magazines on the table next to me held my interest for very long. My mind kept going back to images of Doug laid out on an operating table, cut open.

"Mrs. Branton?" A woman dressed in blue scrubs called my name from the doorway. Well, my soon-to-be name.

I shot out of my chair and invaded her personal space. "How's he doing? When can I see him?" Twisting my hands in front of me, I bombarded the woman with questions. "How bad was it?"

She held her hands up and waved them to calm me down. "One thing at a time."

"Okay," I blurted out loudly. I swallowed, following with a much softer, "okay."

"I'm Dr. Huff. I wish we were meeting on better terms." Her weak smile set me on edge. "Your husband came in with multiple skull fractures." She glanced at the woman behind me, then lowered her voice as she said, "We tried to control the bleeding and the swelling as best we could, but—"

"So it's bad?" I interrupted. "Will he be able to lead a normal life?" What little food I had left in my stomach threatened to make a repeat appearance. What if he never walked or talked again? He could be wheelchair bound for the rest of his life. Maybe even stuck in a bed. I'd do whatever it took to give him a happy life.

She gave two infinitesimal shakes of her head. "I said we tried the best we could, but we were unable to stop the hemorrhaging, and the damage to his brain was too extensive."

I swallowed down the bile that rose. "So..."

"I'm sorry, Mrs. Branton. We weren't able to save your husband."

To the doctor's right, Lora appeared in the doorway and stopped in her tracks, eyes wide. She must have heard what the doctor just told me.

"Josie? Oh my God!" She brushed past the doctor to embrace me.

I collapsed into Lora's arms. My chest squeezed tight, making breathing difficult.

"He... He... He's gone!" I managed between gasps.

Lora patted my back and rubbed soothing circles. It did little to alleviate the hole in my chest. A piece of me was missing, my other half ripped viciously from my side.

We hadn't even begun our life together, and it was already over.

4

The sun warmed my face and the breeze brushed along my neck, swirling the tiny hairs at the nape that had escaped the bobby pins of my updo. Goosebumps rose along my shoulders and arms. I smoothed the hairs back into place, trying not to fidget too much while the pastor quoted scripture by the graveside. I'd already disturbed his beautiful speech with my ill-contained sobs and the grotesque sounds of me blowing my nose.

He'd swept his gaze in my direction, his gray eyes feigning understanding. I knew he didn't appreciate my dramatics, but dammit, my fiancé rested not ten feet from me. The life I'd envisioned with him was squashed like the wet grass trapped under my black high heels.

His sleek, mahogany casket stood suspended above a hole in the ground. The earth would soon swallow him up, and I'd be left alone.

I shrugged as another chill took over my body. The day

started out warm and promised a balmy eighty degrees, yet here I sat, shivering from a draft.

Valerie leaned closer from my right side and whispered, "Stop moving. You're giving me anxiety."

Maybe the frigid temperature came from her direction. If the woman possessed a heart, it was made completely of ice. Her hideous lavender dress wasn't exactly appropriate for the occasion, and I knew she had only come to take advantage of the free food that would follow.

Lora sat on my other side, her eyes as red as mine felt. She'd been a true friend through and through. She grasped my hand and gave it a reassuring squeeze. "Don't listen to the bitch. She's just jealous she's not the one being lowered into the ground so she can be the center of attention."

Valerie leaned around me, murder in her eyes.

On the other side of Valerie, my mom arched a brow, silently asking me what the fuck was going on. I didn't have an answer for her. Not where my two friends were concerned.

I choked on my laughter, thankful for the distraction from my grief, but knew I needed to put an end to their bickering before they made a scene, no matter how much I agreed with Lora. That woman's comments were gold.

"Both of you, stop!" I snapped. My words weren't exactly whispered, earning me a sharp look from the pastor. "Sorry." I slunk down in my seat and gave my friends the evil eye for getting me in trouble.

My mom snorted, trying to cover up her own laughter.

At least Helen was behaving herself on the other side of Lora. I gave her a thankful, yet teary smile.

While my attention was focused on Helen, someone caressed my forearm. I bit back a scream and shot a look at Valerie.

"What?" She shifted away when I narrowed my eyes at her.

I wrapped my affected arm around my midsection. "Did you just touch me?"

She had the nerve to look offended. "Why don't you ask Lora over there? It wasn't me."

The pastor cleared his throat, his eyes sweeping over the three of us. "Let us bow our heads in prayer." He closed his eyes and lowered his head.

Bowing my head, I clasped my hands in my lap and listened to the soothing words being spoken. I tried to forget the people sitting around me and focused solely on the pastor's words of reverence.

My soul ached for closure. I wished I could have spoken with Doug one last time. Did I tell him I loved him before he'd walked out our front door that night?

I couldn't remember. Guilt ate at me. It festered, leaving me feeling weak. Our last phone conversation, I'd gotten mad at him and hung up. His last interaction with me held no love, happiness, or even understanding. What if I could have saved him?

The pressure in my head from crying became unbearable. A pounding took up residence behind my eyes. I pinched the bridge of my nose, trying to relieve some of the pain, but it was no use. This pain would always be a constant in my body in some form or fashion. I just needed to get used to it.

Another tingling sensation passed over the skin on my

other arm. I jumped up from my seat, not able to hold back the shriek as I slapped at my arm.

The pastor's cold, gray eyes cast judgement. He narrowed them as he calculated his response. "Is there something the matter, miss?"

Miss. His last word a slap in the face.

I smoothed out the front of my sleeveless black dress and avoided his gaze, instead, focusing on the ground. Anywhere but his judgmental stare or the casket that lay beside him. Maybe I was losing it. The hospital had referred me to a therapist, but I wasn't ready to talk to a stranger about my problems.

The pastor strolled over. He laid a gentle hand on my shoulder. "I know these times are hard, but this too shall pass."

I shrugged off both his hand and concern and turned to the final resting place for Doug. "Can we just get this over with, please?"

"Of course. Of course." He finished up his elaborate speech and then turned to the funeral director, giving him a nod.

My mother stood up and wrapped an arm around me as the casket lowered into the grave. Her lended strength helped keep me upright.

I wished my father were here. Even though we'd had our differences, I still missed him. Soon, Doug and Dad would get to see each other. An unexpected meeting, for sure.

My eyes burned. I'd cried myself out of tears, or so I thought. Wetness crept to the edge and threatened to spill over. How many more tears would I shed?

The pastor said a blessing over the casket, his lips tight. He was ready to be through with me. I didn't blame him. I couldn't stand myself right now, either.

With the beautiful mahogany box settled at the bottom of the grave, my world blurred around the edges. A single flower was placed in my hand. The words from whoever had given it to me but a distant noise.

I wiped my eyes with the back of my hand and whispered my own little prayer. Doug was a good man. I hoped he found peace in the afterlife.

My hand hovered over the hole in the ground, clutching the stem tightly. This was goodbye. I released the flower and watched as the breeze picked up and nearly swept it away from the grave. It hit the edge and tumbled down into the dank, dark earth, resting beside the casket.

"It's time to go." Helen wrapped her hand around mine and tried to lead me away, but I yanked my fingers from her grasp.

"No. I'm staying until the end." I sniffed hard to keep my nose from running. "He would have wanted it that way."

The pastor grabbed my elbow. "Miss, we don't do that around here anymore."

"The hell we don't!" I jerked my elbow away from him and growled. "I'll stay until the last crumb of dirt is smoothed out, or I'll delay payment to the funeral home."

The funeral director's eyes widened. He pushed the pastor and my mother out of the way and stood too close for comfort, adjusting his black suit jacket. "There'll be no need for that. You stay as long as you like." He clasped one of my hands between both of his and smiled. "I'll even leave a few chairs for you and your family.

My mother stepped between us, throwing in her southern charm. "That's very kind of you, sir. Bless your heart."

Everyone knew *bless your heart* was the southern equivalent to fuck you. The funeral director apparently understood my mother loud and clear.

He stuttered out a "You're welcome, ma'am," before backing away and leaving.

I turned to find only Lora standing behind me. Valerie and Helen were nowhere in sight.

"Valerie," Lora waved her hand in the air animatedly, "had a *thing*."

"And Helen?" I asked.

"She needed to get back home to the kids before one of them put peanut butter in the toaster again." Lora forced a smile. "I'm here for you and so is your mom. We'll stay with you as long as you need us."

"That's right." My mom gently pushed on both of my shoulders and ushered me backwards into a chair. She claimed the chair next to me that Valerie had originally put up a fuss to have. Lora sat to my right.

Workers began clearing the other chairs and the clinks and grinding of heavy machinery filled the air.

The backhoe gradually filled in the hole one scoop at a time. With each pile of dirt, my eyes grew more red. Large wet spots darkened my black dress where my tears had fallen and merged together into one big mess.

I stayed until the shovels evened out the dirt. The

gravestone wouldn't be ready for another week or two. I didn't need a marker to tell me where the other half of my soul rested. I'd always know.

As I said my final goodbyes and my mother helped me to her car, I felt her hand resting on my shoulder. When I glanced at her hand, it wasn't there. The sensation evaporated as quickly as it had came.

No, my mother's hand was on my lower back, guiding me along the grassy hills of the cemetery.

So what had I felt on my shoulder?

5

Little tendrils of dread wrapped around heart, sinking in deeper than the day before. I rested a hand on my chest and breathed through the panic attack I felt creeping in.

No amount of time or space could have prepared me for going through Doug's things. Whether we'd only been together for five years or fifty, I guaranteed it would've still felt like someone clawing a hole into my chest.

For the past few days, I'd started the same ritual: open a box, pause at the items within, close it up, and decide to start on something else.

Today, I would be stronger. I would get through at least one box instead of retreating to my inner thoughts and turmoil.

I knelt down by a box on the floor, slid my finger under one of the flaps, and lifted up. Inside, Doug's *Funko Pop!* collection stared back at me. We'd scoured video game stores trying to find all of his favorite characters.

I pulled out one of the pristine boxes. The mother of dragons rested inside her plastic and cardboard home, forever trapped. Doug had refused to take any of them out. He claimed one day they would be worth a lot of money.

Thump.

My shoulders tensed as I relived the nightmare of the night of Doug's accident. Those damn shutters wouldn't shut up that night, but this noise didn't sound like it came from outside.

I turned to find a paperback on the floor. The bookshelf behind me held books on every available surface, some stacked up to help fit all of them on there.

How in the world had a book fallen off of a shelf packed tighter than a camel's ass in a sandstorm? I eyed the paperback wearily, noticing the title. *Game of Thrones*, one of his favorite series to read and reread. He kept trying to get me to start the novels, but I was never one to read the books if I'd already seen the movie or show.

Reaching down to pick up the book, a cold chill swept through me, raising every hair on my body. I shivered and retreated a safe distance. What if the shutters, the book, and the odd feelings were all connected?

I didn't believe in ghosts but the evidence was starting to stack up pretty high.

Suddenly, I no longer wanted to be alone in this big house. If ghosts were real, could they harm a person? I wasn't sticking around to find out.

I grabbed my phone off a nearby table and raced down the stairs to the living room. My brain went into overdrive, thinking of all the reasons a ghost could be haunting my new house. Well, my new-to-me house.

There was a show Doug used to make me watch. *Ghost Whisperer*. I wondered what flavor of apparition lingered in this space? Were they murdered? Did they perhaps have unfinished business? They apparently loved to read.

Lora's number flashed across the screen of my phone. I swiped my finger across the glass and pushed the phone to my ear.

"Lora?" I'd just made up my mind to call her and here she was calling me instead. Creepy things were happening around here.

"Hey, Josie. I... I wanted to call to check up on you. See if there's anything you need."

"Actually, do you think you could come over? I've got a little problem." I bit my lip and hoped she didn't press me for more information. She needed to actually be here, to feel what was going on, and to see the book laying on the floor.

"Sure. I'll be right over, babe." She disconnected without so much as a *why*. It was one of the reasons I loved her.

"So, you're telling me that book just jumped off the shelf?" She rested a hand on her hip, the other one pointing accusingly at the innocent-looking paperback on the floor.

All I could do was nod. I wouldn't have believed it if I hadn't seen it, well... *heard* it.

I picked at my nails and looked over at the shelf. "You don't believe me."

"Actually, I do." She rested her other hand on her hip and turned to me, concerned. "I know you don't believe in ghosts, so if something has you spooked this much then there's gotta be something going on." She picked up the book, and I noticed a slight shiver race down her spine.

"Did you feel something?" I asked.

She stared at the book in her hand, paralyzed. Her fingers finally appeared to work, and she dropped the book, letting out a tiny, high-pitched squeak.

"Outside. Now!" She grabbed my arm and tugged me along with her until we'd made it all the way through the house and were standing on the porch. "We need answers, and I only know one place that can help."

"What are you talking about?" I reached for the front door's handle, and she slapped my hand.

"Oh, no, no, no." She shimmied in between me and the door, blocking the way. "You can't go back in there."

"But I need to get my purse if we're going to go somewhere."

"Fine, but be quick about it." She opened the door and watched me the entire time.

I lifted my purse from the couch and slung the strap over my shoulder, waving my hands in the air. "See? Nothing bad happened."

The shattering of glass echoed from the stairwell, and I hightailed it out to the porch like lightning had struck my ass.

"Nothing bad happened, right?" Lora arched a well manicured eyebrow, a sarcastic remark just hanging on her tongue.

"Hush, you." I hopped down the stairs. "Your car or mine?"

"We'll take mine. I know where we're going."

I'D NEVER BEEN to an occult shop, so I wasn't exactly sure what to expect. Lora's open-mindedness had drawn me to her like a magnet ever since grade school. She'd been there for me longer than Valerie and Helen. She also proved time and time again to be my most reliable friend. If she believed this store with the blacked-out windows could help, then I would give it a shot.

Herbs and incense enveloped me in a calming embrace when I walked through the door. The dimly lit store gave off a slightly creepy vibe, but my gut could ignore it in the pursuit of a ghost-free residence.

Shelves loitered in every available nook and cranny. Some shelves were packed full of books about crystals, divination, and paganism. I stepped around another shelf to move farther through the store which held bowls upon bowls of different types of crystals in varying colors. An incense display full of tall, thin boxes, along with one incense stick lit on the top, would be the reason for the smell that greeted me at the door.

"You sure about this?" I questioned Lora.

We both walked slowly to the back. The sign on the front had said open, but doubt settled in the back of my mind when we didn't encounter anyone the whole way through.

I startled when beads rustled around a doorway and a

woman in what I could only describe as hippie skirts came waltzing out barefoot. Her long, brown hair fell down to her waist and bangles jingled on her wrists as she came closer.

"Good evening," she said softly. "How may I help you?"

My mouth flopped open and closed, unsure of where to begin. How did one go about confessing to a stranger they had a ghost in their house? "I'm not sure if—"

"Tamsin, my friend here has a ghost problem," Lora cut in. Quite rudely, might I add. I sent her an evil side-eye, but kept my mouth shut.

She smiled back sweetly, then looked to the woman she'd called Tamsin.

"Ghosts, you say?" Tamsin ran a finger along the edge of her counter, then her hand dipped below the surface. When her hand resurfaced, she held within it a single business card. She canted her head, regarding Lora. "Your friend is right, though. I can't help her, but I know someone who can."

"You do?" Hope swelled in my chest like an over-inflated balloon. "Who?"

She set her dark brown eyes on me, a twinkle in them. "Mr. Lore should be able to rid you of your ghost problem. I've heard nothing but good things about him." She flicked the edge of the card. It disappeared from her fingers and reappeared in my hand.

An involuntary gasp bubbled up as I stared at the card in my palm. Sebastian Lore, Clairvoyant Medium.

"A medium? Really?" I asked in disbelief, but we *were* talking about a ghost. What solution did I honestly think I would receive in an occult shop? It wasn't like there was some electronic device I could plug into my wall that scared ghosts away.

Tamsin rested her hand on my wrist, a warmth radiating from her palm, and gave me a small smile. "Getting rid of a ghost is not easy work. You must trust your instincts as well as the medium helping you." Her eyes twinkled mischievously. "I have a feeling you're in for a big surprise."

"A big surprise? What are you talking about?" I dropped the card in my purse, mentally wondering if this woman held all her faculties.

"If I told you, then it wouldn't be a surprise." Tamsin chuckled. "Good luck with your ghost problem."

Lora covered her mouth and looked away to hide her laughter.

"You think this is funny?" I poked her side, and she yelped. "This is no laughing matter."

Tamsin stepped back to the beaded curtain, preparing to slip behind it when she turned. Her mouth set in a hard line, and her forehead creased. "Once again, your friend is right." She gave a nod and disappeared, beads clinking together in her wake.

The woman's reaction had me wondering how serious I should take this. A wave of dizziness caught me off guard, and I clutched at the counter.

Lora snickered. "Josie, you should see the look on your face. It's like you've seen a... nevermind. Bad joke."

I collected myself before we left. Lora didn't need to know how unsettled the interaction with Tamsin had made me. I pulled the card from my purse as soon as we got in the car and watched the silver lettering of Sebastian's name shimmer in the dying light. The front of the business card was very simplistic. Just the name, what he did, and a phone number to contact him on a black background. I flipped the card over. No picture or anything else. Very mysterious.

"Why don't you call him while I drive you home? Go ahead and get an appointment in case he books up fast." Lora pulled onto the road without a glance in my direction.

The streets of downtown Austin whirled by as fast as my thoughts. "Do you really think this will work? What if my mind is just making up crazy shit because Doug is gone? What if there's nothing wrong with my house?"

"You heard the book fall, you heard that crash in your kitchen, and you and me both felt something off just standing near that damn book." She finally glanced my way and what I saw chilled me to the bone. Her expression trumped the seriousness I'd found on Tamsin's.

Panic replaced any laughter her eyes once held in the shop. She was scared for me. Petrified about whatever haunted my house. This only ratcheted up my anxiety sending my heart into a frantic rhythm.

"You're right." With shaky fingers, I punched the guy's phone number into my phone and pressed it to my ear.

"Of course I'm right," Lora chimed in, her snarky attitude back.

He picked up on the third ring. "Hello?"

"Sebastian?" I asked, wondering if this was a mistake, but I couldn't back out. I needed help.

"This is he. How can I help you?" A smooth, sexy timbre came through the line. I knew that voice. It sounded familiar but I couldn't place it. His name didn't ring a bell either.

"I've got a ghost in my house. I think. I'm not sure. Fuck."
I bit my lip to stop my rambling, then asked, "Can you help...
please?"

"It's what I specialize in. I can set something up and
come take a look at your house." Papers shuffled around.
"How soon do you need me to come out?"

"Now," I blurted out. "Shit. I mean, whatever your
earliest availability is. I'm sorry. My nerves are rattled." I
wiped a sweaty hand on my jeans and switched hands and
ears to do the same with the other.

"I completely understand. Just take a deep breath. We'll
figure all this out, and you can get your life back on track."
The deepness of his voice sparked lustful thoughts as I
imagined him whispering in my ear. I winced, trying to
shake that and other images out of my head. I'd just buried
my fiancé and my libido was dancing the Mamba at the
sound of a stranger's voice. I was more messed up than I
thought.

"So, how soon can you be out?" I couldn't imagine
sleeping in that house alone tonight. Not without figuring
out what - or who - was in my home.

"Hmm." He tapped his nails or a pen against a hard
surface, I wasn't sure which. "I actually have time tonight. I
can come by, get a feel for the place, and see what I'm
working with."

"Tonight? That'd be great!" I replied a little too
enthusiastically.

Lora snickered beside me. "Is it a date?"

"Hush!" I whispered to her.

"What?"

"Not you. Sorry. My friend was trying to talk to me."

"No problem. Text me your address, and I'll be over around nine o'clock, maybe a little later."

"Deal. Thank you, Sebastian!"

"You're welcome." I could hear the smile in his voice, and it set my heart into a flurry of beats. I hadn't felt this alive in days, but I shouldn't feel that way. Not after the death of Doug.

Lora chuckled as she pulled up to my house. "It *is* a date. Your face doesn't know how to lie, does it?" She wiggled her eyebrows at me. "Did he sound like a phone sex operator? Is that why your face is all red?"

"Shut up! It is not a date!"

I stared out the windshield at my beautiful Victorian house as Lora pulled up in my driveway. The house that had betrayed me and made me feel unsafe.

"Lora?" I whined.

"Yes, sweetheart?" Her playful tone was gone.

"Will you stay with me tonight so I'm not all alone?" I turned away from the house and frowned at Lora, waiting for an answer. If she said no, I'd be booking a night at the nearest hotel.

To my relief she nodded. I only hoped we both lived to see the sunrise.

6

Sebastian Lore strolled up my concrete walkway like he owned every cracked square. The streetlight backlit his figure, accentuating the shape of his muscled arms and trim waist.

My mouth watered at the sight of him. I did not expect a demigod to show up at my house at nine o'clock at night, but I guess if anyone could get rid of a ghost, someone like him could. His voice definitely matched his exterior.

"It's not a date, remember?" Lora mocked. She slapped my back. "And you're drooling. Pull it together, woman!"

Leave it to my best friend to knock some sense into me. I closed my mouth and ran a finger over my lips to make sure I wasn't actually drooling. That would have been awkward.

Awkward didn't seem to cover it when the man reached the halo of my porch light and the lamp illuminated his face.

"Oh, dear God in heaven," Lora mumbled beside me.

I murmured a reply back to her. "If that's God, then I need to go to church more often."

"Josie?" Sebastian said, confused.

"Yes?" I managed to squeeze out through my parched throat.

The man before me was none other than the stripper from my bachelorette party.

He stood at the bottom of the porch stairs, staring up with a well aimed smirk. "You never told me your name on the phone." His long legs carried him up the five steps to my porch. He still smelled of incense and smoke like the first time we'd met.

To avoid sniffing him again, I took a step back to give him space, even as my body screamed for me to lean closer. His dark brown hair was messy tonight, half of it covering one of his blue eyes.

"No, I didn't. And you never asked." A tingle ran down my spine, and my skin twitched. What the hell was going on? I resisted the urge to squirm, instead, turning to open the door to my house. "Let's take a look inside. Shall we?"

Lora shook her head as she stepped past me into the house.

My skin tingled for other reasons when Sebastian's cool gaze gave me a once-over on his way in.

Inside, he got down to business. "Where did you first feel the ghost?"

"In my bedroom." My cheeks burned. I'd have to take him up to my room, which had a bed. I knew how that body of his moved in one fluid motion. He'd danced like a sex god at my party. Now, I couldn't get the image of him in my bed out of my mind. Lora would be no help, either. I knew she'd encourage any *adult time* and probably try to join in herself. "It's right this way."

"How'd your wedding go?" he asked from behind me as we ascended the stairs.

I paused mid-staircase, gripping the rail, refusing to turn around. "It didn't." I continued up to my room with awkward, stiff legs.

"Oh. I'm sorry." But he didn't sound sorry.

And I didn't elaborate on the reason why I never got hitched. The pain was still too new, too raw. My heart mourned the loss of a man I loved while my body warred with the thought of releasing some pent up frustrations with the chiseled Adonis following at my heels.

The doorway of my room was the closest I was willing to get to the book in the middle of the floor.

Lora stayed in the hall, shaking out her arms. "All I can think about is what happened when I touched that book."

Sebastian's shoulder brushed mine deliberately as he slipped into my bedroom, glancing over his shoulder to make eye contact. When he turned back around, I admired the tight shirt and the acid washed jeans riding low on his hips.

Sebastian took a deep breath and released it. "Whatever you're doing, Josie, you're pissing off whoever is here."

"What?" My eyes widened, and I looked around him to the book on the floor. "Who's pissed?"

"There is a spirit here, but he's not willing to show himself or tell me anything." Sebastian closed his eyes and squinted like perhaps he needed a better look at the back of his eyelids. Part of me started to wonder if this guy was legit.

I'd barely lived here for a couple weeks, and I had a ghost upset with me?

Lora spoke from behind me. "Yup. My happy ass is gonna stay in the hall. Thanks."

"Shh!" Without opening his eyes, he waved a hand at Lora to be quiet.

I looked back at Lora, and she silently put her hands up and shrugged. My friend trusted this Tamsin, but could I trust her and the guy she suggested?

I didn't go to church often, but something told me I should go this Sunday to repent for my recent activities.

Sebastian opened his eyes and picked up the book. He slowly walked over to the shelf and placed it back in the only available slot. "You sure do love books."

"Reading is—" I watched in horror as one of the books on the very top shelf slowly pushed itself out. "Watch out!"

But my words failed to warn him in time. The hardback plummeted in a flutter of pages, one of the corners jabbing Sebastian square in the forehead as he looked up.

Dropping to a knee, he grabbed his head and his hand came away with blood.

"Oh my goodness!" I rushed to his side.

From recent experience, I knew head wounds bled the most. I placed both my hands on either side of his head and turned him toward the ceiling light to get a better look.

"How bad is it, doc?" he joked with me.

I licked my dry lips and watched those beautiful blues track the movement. "I don't know if you're going to make it. I give you a week tops, maybe two." I'd always hid pain and worry behind humor. "Stay right here."

The bathroom wasn't completely unpacked, but it was close to being the first room done. Showering and using the restroom were two of the more important activities needed in the house. I grabbed a clean washcloth from the linen closet and wet it in the sink, then grabbed the first aid kit from one of the boxes.

Back in my bedroom, I found Sebastian standing. I pointed to my bed and demanded, "Sit."

"Yes, ma'am." He put his hands up and backed away. When his calves hit the mattress, he sank down.

I wiped his hand clean first, then ministered to his forehead. As I dabbed the rag on the bleeding wound, I realized I stood between his spread legs and my chest was at eye level.

Lora piped up. "Uh, I just realized I left something in my car. I'll be right back."

Before I could turn around and protest, Lora disappeared. I returned my attention back to Sebastian and swallowed hard, trying to concentrate on his forehead and not his strong legs on either side of mine.

"I, uh." My tongue felt two times its size. "Your prognosis is improving by the minute."

His charming smirk returned. He had a perfect cupid's bow and the scruff on his cheeks only added to my fantasies.

Focus. I needed to focus.

I heard a zipper and dropped the wet rag onto his jeans. "Oops! I'm so sorry." When I grabbed for the rag, I saw he'd unzipped the first aid kit, not his jeans. I really needed to get my head in a better place.

"It's ok. I thought I'd help you out and get the Band-Aid

ready. It's only going to need a Band-Aid, right?" He looked up at me, and the moment felt more intimate than it should.

What was supposed to be a little first aid treatment was turning into a walking wet dream. I'd never been this turned on in my life, and all I'd done was stand here with a wet rag cleaning his forehead. What was wrong with me?

"Sure." I tried to still the trembling in my hands as I took the opened bandage from him. Holding my breath, I eased the Band-Aid over the skin. I smoothed a finger over the sticky parts to make sure it adhered to his skin. "There you go."

He winced and grabbed my wrist. "Thank you."

"Wait! We forgot antibiotic ointment!" I rummaged through the first aid kit and he grabbed my hand again with a chuckle.

"I'm sure it'll be fine. I don't think books can cause infections."

Lora cleared her throat from the doorway. "You two done or should I go back to my car again?"

Two large steps back, and I was safely out of the reach of temptation. I nodded and avoided looking over at Sebastian. "I'm good."

"Your ghost appears pissed at more than just you." He rubbed close to the Band-Aid and hissed. "That smarts."

"What do you mean?" Lora asked. She still avoided my room like the plague. I wasn't sure how we were going to get through the rest of the night.

"I mean, he threw that book at me. I still didn't get a glimpse of him." Sebastian stood up from my bed and avoided walking near the bookshelf. "He even laughed after he was done."

"He? My ghost is a he?"

"Very much so."

Great. I had a male ghost running around my bedroom. The place where I got undressed and slept. I still didn't know if ghosts could harm me, but what if they could touch me?

I shuddered from head to toe, wondering what I'd gotten myself into by moving into this ancient house.

7

"How the hell do I get rid of this *male* ghost, then?" I'd ventured way too close to the books. Skirting around the bookshelf and the hardback book, I joined Lora in the doorway. "I can't sleep in here knowing there's some sort of guy in my room!"

Sebastian ushered us out into the hallway. "Have you only had issues in this room? Have there been any other rooms in the house where you've felt spiritual activity?"

"No. Well." I nervously rubbed a hand up and down my arm. "About a week ago, one of the shutters on the house came loose during one of the storms. I feel like that's somehow connected."

"It depends on what's holding the spirit to this world." He shrugged. "It could be as simple as a special keepsake or part of the building. I've heard of some houses being haunted because windows were taken and repurposed from another house, and the ghost followed the pieces the builder had taken."

"What? Are you serious?" This house's history spanned decades. No telling how many other ghosts may be lurking in the corners. "I can't even think straight right now. This house is over a hundred years old."

"I have a feeling the shutters aren't a part of it. Perhaps the wind just knocked it loose." He nodded toward the stairs, and we followed. "Taking that into account, let's go with the assumption the ghost is attached to only that room or something in it. I'd suggest sleeping somewhere else."

"I've got the sectional in the living room. Lora and I can sleep on that tonight."

"I'm glad you have your friend staying with you." He flashed me a grin that sent need burning along every available nerve ending in my body. "I wouldn't want you to be alone."

Damnit, Sebastian's devilish smile seemed to promise so many things in one simple gesture. He made me want to push Lora onto the porch and confess I'd be scared and alone in this big, empty house.

Then the guilt hit. It festered and ate its way through my gut like acid, making me sick to my stomach. Was it wrong of me to think of another man so soon after my fiancé's death? Doug would want me to be happy. There was an appropriate mourning period, but I wasn't sure what acceptable time length I needed to wait. Pretty sure it wasn't a few days.

"Thank you." We shuffled into the living room, and I took a seat on the couch. "I still need to know how to get rid of this ghost."

"You can start with a few simple things. Burning sage to cleanse the area and remove any negative energy may get rid of him." Sebastian propped himself against the arm of the couch and watched me closely.

Lora grinned behind her hand. I knew as soon as he left, I wouldn't escape Lora's barrage of questions. She took a seat on the other side of the sectional, mentally eating popcorn and watching the show.

"You're telling me it could be as simple as burning a plant, and *poof*, no ghost?" I rested my hands in my lap to keep myself from reaching out to him. I'd never felt this compelled to be close to a man before, not after first meeting him. This spark started the first moment I opened the door at Valerie's house. We'd locked eyes and something had passed between us.

"Yup, but just in case." He pulled up his phone and started thumbing through screens. "I've got some other things scheduled the next couple of days, but I can come out on Thursday, and we can do a seance."

My eyes widened. "A seance?"

"Yes." He started typing information on his phone. I leaned over and saw him putting in a calendar entry. "If you have a couple other friends you can invite over, then we can make a circle and try to pull the ghost into the circle, see what's keeping him here, and then help him pass on."

Would my friends think I'd totally lost it? Lora embraced all things outside of the box. She'd be down for the seance. Helen or Valerie would never let me hear the end of it. I arched an eyebrow in question at Lora.

"Helen probably wouldn't care," Lora supplied, not disappointing me.

We both knew Valerie to be the judgy one in our cluster of friends.

"Then it's set," Sebastian said, tucking his phone into his back pocket as he stood. He gave me a wink. "Try the sage. If it doesn't work, text me."

Like a good hostess, I walked to the door and showed Sebastian out. Lora stayed inside while I stepped onto the porch.

"I'm not going to lie," Sebastian started, "but I'm hoping the sage doesn't work. I'd like to see you again. I'm sorry it didn't work out with you and that guy."

My heart turned to goo and slid into my stomach. I never elaborated on what happened with Doug, and it wasn't any of his business. Whatever this was between us probably wouldn't go anywhere. Sebastian's face and body put Greek gods to shame while I looked like one of the peasants that paid homage at his temple. Though, a dalliance with him would be welcomed. Even Greek gods came to earth for a little fun before returning to Mount Olympus.

"If it's too soon, I understand. I know you were supposed to get married, but..." Sebastian trailed off. He must have read my facial expressions all wrong.

"No, no." I sucked up an ounce of courage, daring myself to touch him, and rested a hand on his shoulder. The muscles felt so hard beneath my touch, I almost swooned. "I'd like that."

He turned toward the street to hide his smile. When he looked back, he placed a hand over mine. With my hand trapped between his strong shoulder and warm palm, I felt my face flush.

"I'll see you in a few days, Josie."

After Sebastian left, I entered the house in a daze. I dropped to the couch and stared at the door with a dreamy sigh.

"Earth to Josie. Hello, Josie?" Lora stood in front of me and waved her hand around, but I barely saw her. Instead, Sebastian's smiling face before he ambled to his car flashed across my vision. "Are you going to tell me what's up between you and the stripper?"

That question snapped me out of my hallucination. "What?"

"You and Sebastian. You two seemed pretty cozy up there in your room." She sat down beside me and bumped into me.

"Be nice or I'll cut your purple tips off your hair in your sleep!" I warned. If I didn't set up a good threat to establish some boundaries, she'd never shut up about Sebastian.

Lora squinted her eyes and pursed her lips. "You wouldn't."

"Guess we'll find out soon enough." I winked, and Lora scowled more. "Anyways, I was only tending to the injury on his head." Which was the truth. Nothing happened. We'd both stayed fully clothed, and I'd only wiped the blood off of his head and put a Band-Aid over the wound.

If I didn't have any reason to feel guilty, why did I? I was pretty sure the date I had in three days had something to do with it. Even if that date consisted of a seance.

"I'd bet money it was more than his head that hurt after he walked out of your house." Lora guffawed. "Now, do you think it's safe to use your shower?" She dangled her travel pack from her fingers. This woman always made sure she was prepared.

"If the ghost is only holing up in my room, you should be." I trudged to the stairs, not overly excited about having to go to the upper level of the house. "Follow me. I'll show you where it is."

The bathroom door looked innocent enough, but I still hesitated before turning the old crystal knob. Inside, I flipped the the switch, and fluorescent light flooded the room from three frosted sconces.

I jerked the curtain back from the clawfoot tub, screaming even though there wasn't anything behind it.

"You okay, girl?" Lora laughed at my expense and pushed the door open wider. "This is nice. I like the black and white tiles."

"I'm good. Just a little on edge."

"Understandable. Um, Josie?" Lora's tone rose in pitch, making me pause in closing the curtain.

"Yeah?" I feared what I'd find when I turned around. Did she see another ghost? Was something on the verge of falling off the shelf in the corner and I was the next victim of abuse?

"Did you get all artistic on your mirror this morning?" She dropped her toiletry bag on the floor and took a step back just as I turned to look at her.

When I glanced up at the mirror, a red heart drawn in lipstick stood out against all the black and white reflected in the background. "What the actual fuck?"

I'd never draw on my mirror. Especially not a heart and definitely not after the death of my fiancé.

Lora backed up more, and I followed her. "Go, go, go!" I

pushed her into the hall, and we both took the stairs down two at a time. If I were more agile, I would have slid down the banister. "The second floor is off limits!"

Even as I said it, I wondered if it was only the second floor I should be concerned with or if the whole damn house was teeming with ghosts.

8

A strange, earthy smell woke me the next morning. I twisted to sit up on the couch, and my back popped in several places. "Oh, damn. I'm too young to feel this old."

"You're not that old, Josie." Lora appeared in the living room doorway with a bundle of small twigs on fire - well, smoldering. She waved the smoke around my front door, then proceeded to do the same to each of the casement windows.

"I know this goes without saying, but what the fuck are you doing?"

"Smudging." Lora said the one word so matter-of-factly, like it explained everything.

When she saw my brows scrunch up, she shook her head.

"You didn't listen to Sebastian last night, did you?" She waltzed over to the opening to the hallway. Lines of smoke curled past the flowered wallpaper and the crown molding, disappearing at the ceiling. "He said we could try sage to get rid of the negative energy in the house, thus banishing the ghost. I ran out this morning while you slept and grabbed a couple bundles. I've done the first floor. I was about to head upstairs, but now that you're awake, you can go with me."

"We have to go back upstairs?" I gawked. "I don't know if that's wise."

"What isn't wise is sitting on the couch all day and doing nothing. We need to be proactive in getting rid of this ghost, or you're going to have to move again." She pointed the smoking stick toward the stairs. "Come on. The ghost isn't going to evict itself!"

"Fine, fine," I grumbled. My hips hurt from sleeping on the couch. How did Doug ever think this couch was comfortable to sleep on?

Upstairs, Lora waved her magic stick around more. The cloying smell made me cough. "Does it have to smell like that?"

"Maybe if you were being more positive it wouldn't affect you." Lora bit her lip to keep from laughing.

"Touche." My index finger waved in the air, striking an invisible cymbal.

We finished all the rooms upstairs, and then went down to the kitchen to make coffee and figure out lunch since I'd slept so late.

"Coffee smells so much better than sage." I sucked in a lungful of the heavenly scent as it brewed.

We chatted about everything but ghosts, waiting for the pot to get about halfway full before we each stole a cup.

I took a hearty sip from my mug, then nearly spit it out when a series of crashes came from upstairs. "Um... Lora?"

"I don't think the sage helped," she deadpanned.

I shook my head. "I don't either." I demurely took another sip of coffee from my oversized Disney Stitch mug. This day would definitely require copious amounts of coffee. "We have to go upstairs, don't we?"

"Mm hmm," Lora said with her lips around the edge of her cup. One of my favorite mugs, complete with scales and a mermaid tail for the handle. I had quite the collection.

"Fine." I set my mug on the counter. "Let's get this over with."

The stairs creaked no matter how much I leaned on the carved banister. I didn't need to alert the ghost that we were coming to check on the noise, but the ghost - being a supernatural being - probably already knew we were on our way.

Lora let out a huff and stormed up the stairs past me. "You're going to take two months to get up these stairs, and by then the ghost is going to have taken over the whole house."

I picked up the pace and nearly ran into the back of her. She'd stopped in the doorway to my bedroom, her hand on the door frame. "Josie, I think we're going to need to call Sebastian."

"Why?" I shouldered past her. The hardwood floors were littered with every single book from my shelf. The bookshelf hung at an angle from the anchor I'd put in the wall to prevent it from falling on anyone.

To add insult to injury, all of my blankets, pillows, and bed sheets were ripped from my bed and scattered around the room.

"I have a feeling the ghost wasn't trying to read before bed." Lora snorted.

"You think?" I had the phone from my back pocket pressed to my ear before I could make it to the top of the stairs. "Sebastian? We have a problem."

The scene in my bedroom both caused laughter to bubble up as well a bile. It would have been comical if it'd happened any other way, but a spiritual being had violated my sanctuary, the place I was supposed to feel the safest.

I explained everything to Sebastian and he said he'd be right over. Lora and I didn't have to wait long before his car pulled up to park in the driveway next to Lora's.

He breezed into the house with efficient steps. "I came as soon as I could." His stomach growled, and he looked down sheepishly. "I skipped lunch to be here."

"I'll go grab us something to eat while y'all figure out a way to expel our unwanted guest," Lora piped up. She clutched her keys tightly, ready to bolt.

I couldn't blame her. If I had the choice of staying here or getting out of the house to get food, I'd choose food every single time.

"Here." Sebastian threw a twenty at her. "I'll cover part of it."

"Thanks, cutie!" She pocketed the money with a nervous laugh and booked it to her car.

Once in my bedroom, Sebastian surveyed the damage. "You know, it could be worse." He pushed the bookshelf back and began to reshelf the books on the floor.

"Don't worry about the books. I can clean those up later."

I waved a hand and motioned to the boxes. "Maybe we could move those out of the room so he has less stuff to destroy?"

"That could work." Sebastian picked up one of the heavier boxes, and I guided him to a completely empty room at the back of the house.

We both worked to get the boxes moved. I secretly hoped the ghost wouldn't touch anything in that room. There was no proof yet that the ghost only wanted to destroy my bedroom, but I kept my fingers crossed.

I stacked a box on top of a pile in one corner. Sebastian came up behind me and helped me push it all the way onto the top box.

"Thanks." I crossed my arms and ducked around his body to go grab another box.

"You're welcome. Um, Josie?"

I halted in my tracks and turned. "Yeah?"

"Why do you have boxes with *Doug* written all over them?" He used his foot to push a box beside the growing stack.

The jig was up. I knew sooner or later he might start asking questions. I didn't know why I thought I could keep Doug's death from him, even if the only thing that happened between us was a lap dance. "I... Doug was my fiancé."

"Yeah? And you two didn't get married." Sebastian advanced on me. "That doesn't explain why you still have his things. Shouldn't he have gotten them by now?"

I backed up and bumped into the wall, flattening myself against it. Nervous energy thrummed through my veins. His nearness did strange things to my insides, even with the hint of anger at my dead fiancé boiling to the surface. But he didn't know Doug was dead.

"He can't exactly come and pick his things up." I shuddered as Sebastian's breath fanned over my face.

"Do you need me to help put all of his shit on the lawn?" He flattened his palm on the wall beside me and leaned in closer. "Because I can help you with that."

"Doug can't get his things because he was in a car accident."

Sebastian pulled back, surprised. "I didn't know."

"No, you didn't, because I didn't tell you. He'll never be able to retrieve all of the things in those boxes, because..." I closed my eyes and choked down a sob. "Because he passed away."

"Shit." Sebastian shoved his fingers into his hair and gripped tight, turning away from me to string together a long slew of curses. "I didn't know. I swear. Look." He dropped his hands to his side. "You should have let me know. I wouldn't have come on to you like that had I known you were going through such a tough time."

Part of this blame rested on my shoulders. I should've told him about Doug. I shouldn't have given him such strong signals yesterday when tending to his forehead. But damn him for coming into my life and turning it upside down. Yes, he looked good, but for some unknown reason a part of his soul called to mine.

My relationship with Doug had been a slow burn. We'd started our relationship when an old friend of mine set us up on a blind date. I'd been reluctant from the get-go. He'd wooed me for over a year before I finally committed to a relationship with him. I'd always held a piece of me back, afraid to get hurt. It wasn't until he'd proposed that I'd broken down all those walls and let myself love him wholeheartedly.

In the end, he still broke my heart. He'd left me, just not in the way I had originally feared.

"Wait..." Sebastian rushed from the room.

I chased after him as he ran into my bedroom. "Sebastian. What are you doing?"

He looked around. The room was more spacious with most of the boxes gone. "When did you say all of this started?"

"It started... Well, I thought the shutters were the beginning of it all. It just felt off that they'd come loose so easily."

"That was before Doug passed?" He scratched his head. I saw him trying to put two and two together.

"Yes, the shutters were the night he went out and..." I covered my mouth and swallowed hard before continuing, "...never came home."

"I still don't think that first event is connected to all of this." He gestured to the chaos around us. "This seems too personal. You also mentioned something on your bathroom mirror."

"Yes, a heart drawn in lipstick."

Sebastian whipped around to look at me, his gaze locked with mine. With a weighted gravity, he said, "What if the spirit haunting your house is your dead fiancé?"

9

Lora peeked through the bedroom door, waving around fast food bags in her hands. "Honey, I'm home!" she sing-songed. Her face crumpled as soon as she saw the fresh tears welling in my eyes, ready to join the tears already streaking down my face. Despite her fear of the bedroom, she came into the room, set the bags on the floor, and pulled me into her arms. "Oh no, sweetie. What's the matter?"

"It couldn't be, could it?" I questioned both her and the universe. Doug wouldn't haunt our new house and scare me to death, would he? He couldn't. He'd be decent enough to leave me in peace to mourn his loss.

But what if he hadn't?

"Couldn't be what?" She leaned back to take in my tear stained face.

"Doug." Words failed me. I could only manage the one without bursting into tears again. How could I explain to Lora what Sebastian had just suggested?

Disbelief still weighed heavily on my shoulders. With the age of the house, it was more believable that we had a ghost of an older variety than a newly dead one loitering around because he couldn't move on.

"Josie just told me about her fiancé and his passing." Sebastian paused, trying to tread lightly. "What if... the spirit causing all of this destruction is none other than Doug himself?"

Lora gasped and clutched her hand to her chest. "That bastard!"

"Lora!" I chastised, smacking her arm.

"What? I never liked him much anyway." She grimaced and turned to Sebastian. "Now I know why the sage didn't work."

Sebastian turned to hide his smile, but not quick enough. Lora could be a piece of work, and he was getting a taste of her brand of crazy.

I nudged Lora. "Go get me a tissue or something, please." Anything to keep her out of this conversation.

She pulled out a wrinkled up Kleenex from her pants and waved it at me. "Here"

"You keep tissues in your pocket?" I leaned away from her outstretched hand. "Eww! Is it used?"

"No, it's not used. I just like to... nevermind." She shoved it into my hand. "Here. Use it."

I inspected the wrinkled mass. It didn't appear to have anything stuck to it, so I unfolded it, smoothed it out, and dabbed carefully around my eyes.

"What happened to that Ouija board you bought last year?" Lora asked.

Not this again. Lora, Helen, Valerie, and I had gotten drunk last year on Halloween and made Helen's husband run out and buy us a Ouija board. Between the booze and everyone moving the planchette, we'd determined there was someone who needed us to vacuum their home. And another spirit who was trapped in their basement. That one was interesting. I still pegged Valerie for that *special visit*. She had a sick mind. All in all, we knew it was a joke, but drunk us didn't care.

I pinned Lora with a stare. "You can't be serious."

"Oh, I'm dead serious." She cringed, sucking in a breath through her teeth. "Damnit. Too soon."

"Actually, a Ouija board might do the trick." Sebastian paused, his head cocked to the side as if listening for something. He closed his eyes, his long, dark lashes resting against his cheeks.

In that moment, I decided I'd steal a glance uninterrupted. Sharp cheekbones blended into sensual lips. My gaze froze on his perfectly shaped mouth. I'd meant to check out the rest of him, but the only thought left in my mind were those lips and how they would feel pressed against my own.

His baby blues shot open and caught me red handed. I looked from his eyes to his lips, watching one corner lift up knowingly. He didn't call me out on it. "If the spirit doesn't want to show himself, maybe he'll be okay with communicating through the board."

"That is a terrible idea," I said, still transfixed with my own wandering thoughts.

"I think it's a great idea," Lora countered loudly. "Oh, I

saw a box in the living room that said board games!" She hurried out the door, a woman on a mission.

I groaned and raked a hand down my face. "You just had to encourage her."

"No, it really is a good idea." He sauntered my way, sure of himself and his power over me. "There are numerous ways to contact the spirit world to get answers."

"I think we're asking for trouble." We were having two different conversations. One with our spoken words and another with our body language. I wasn't sure if my statement referred to the Ouija board or this chemistry that kept igniting between us whenever we were left alone in a room for more than ten seconds, but either way, those words rang true.

"I found it!" Lora held the board game box above her head as she traipsed into my bedroom. A moment of surprise crossed her face when her feet connected with the fast food bags. She tried to maneuver to avoid smashing the food, but failed, only to nose-dive onto the hardwood floors, hands thrown out in front of her. The box took flight, soaring through the air.

Sebastian, quick on his feet, caught the box. He set it down on the bed and knelt beside Lora. "Are you okay?"

Lora sat up and examined her hands. "Who the fuck moved the bags into the middle of the doorway?"

Sebastian and I regarded each other. We both knew neither one of us had touched those bags.

"It wasn't us," I said. "Maybe the ghost moved them?"

"Fucking spiritual pranksters," she grumbled as

Sebastian helped her to stand. "I'm done with this ghost. Let's get this over with."

I plucked the box from my bed, and we filed down to the living room.

Lora pulled the ottoman over to the bend in the sectional. I sat where the two pieces of the couch met, and Lora and Sebastian sat on either side.

"Are there any rules to doing this?" I knew getting drunk probably wasn't in our best interest if we wanted results.

"There are a few tips that will help," Sebastian explained, scooting a little closer to me. "One of us will need to be the leader in this. Basically the person in charge that will ask the questions to the spirits and is allowed to talk."

"Allowed to talk?" Lora scoffed. "Are you saying the rest of us have to be quiet? If that's the case, I want to be the leader." She threw her hand up in the air as if we were in school and the teacher had asked for volunteers.

"Lora." I ground my teeth together, trying not to roll my eyes. It took extreme effort. "Sebastian knows more than both of us. You probably don't even remember using the Ouija board back in October. You were drunker than a skunk."

"Well, when you put it like that." She slouched down, sulking and licking her wounds. She'd get over it. We needed an expert to guide us.

"That's settled then. You two should remain quiet." Sebastian opened the box and set the Ouija board on the ottoman with the planchette "Lora, you could be our note taker."

"Do I get to talk?"

"Sadly, no. You'd get to write down whatever we find out and help us to remember things later."

Lora huffed, standing up from the couch. "Fine. Let me go get something to write on." She dragged her feet all the way out of the room.

Once Lora was back, and we were all settled again, Sebastian placed the tips of his fingers from one hand on the planchette. "Now, Josie. Put your fingers on the other side, just like mine. Everyone will need to clear their mind. Quiet all of your thoughts and open yourself up. Focus on the Ouija board and the external environment around you."

I gave a nod, keeping my mouth shut. Color me impressed when Lora did the same.

Sebastian took a deep, calming breath. "I feel like he's followed us down," he whispered softly. He looked around the room. "What is your name?"

My gaze laser-focused on the planchette, I waited for it to move, but nothing happened.

"Why are you here?" Sebastian asked.

Still, the planchette remained unmoving.

Sebastian cracked his neck and rolled his shoulders. "Maybe they need a yes or no answer."

Following the rules, I remained silent, merely giving a nod in agreement.

Lora doodled little flowers in the corner of her notepad, barely paying attention. I wanted to smack her hand, but I knew angering her would only make her talk when she shouldn't.

"Were you killed in this house?" Sebastian asked the open space around us.

The planchette quivered beneath our fingers, unreleased tension building up by the second. I was afraid the thing was going to fly out the door.

"I think we struck a nerve." He cleared his throat.

"I'd say so." I let out a squeak. My free hand flew up and covered my lips. I mouthed a *sorry* to Sebastian.

The trembling of the planchette increased. Suddenly, it flew out from under our fingers, frantically fluttering from letter to letter all on its own.

"Whoa, whoa, whoa..." Sebastian lifted his hand and tracked the movement to each letter. He spoke the letters out loud as they appeared under the round, clear piece of plastic.

"G - E - T - O - U - T - B - O - Y. Hmm." He shuddered from head to toe. "This isn't good. I'm feeling a lot of negative energy from whoever's in this house."

I pitched my voice low, like the ghost couldn't hear me if I whispered. "He just told us to get out."

"Correction. He's telling me to get out. *Get out, boy*. I told you he didn't like me."

Snatching the planchette, I set it right in the middle of the board. "Is this Doug? Let me know if it's you." A single sob escaped, but I managed to hold it together. "I just need to know."

The planchette moved beneath my fingers, tugging my hand to the far corner of the board to stop abruptly on the word *Yes*.

10

I jerked my arm back as if the planchette had caught fire, searing the skin on my fingertips. One word. Three letters. That's all it took to turn my world up on end.

"We need to move the seance up." I jumped to my feet and paced back and forth. "Se-Sebastian," I stuttered, my lips shaking involuntarily. "You need to make him leave. NOW!" My whole body began to shake from adrenaline, anxiety, nerves, fear... you name it, I felt it.

Did I miss Doug? Yes, but this wasn't the way I wanted to reconnect with him. I didn't need him haunting my house, ransacking my furniture, and leaving messages on bathroom mirrors.

"I'm with Josie," Lora added. "Doug is a douche."

"He is *not* a douche," I shot back.

Lora harrumphed. "You want to know why your bachelorette party was at Valerie's house?"

"Valerie just wanted us to see all her fancy house *things*." I wiggled my fingers in the air at my last word, waving Lora's inquiry away afterwards. I didn't want to entertain what her question implied.

"Yes, that was part of it, but Doug asked her to make sure you didn't go out. Valerie told me about it." She stood and approached me cautiously, like I was a wild animal and unpredictable in my actions. "You know how Valerie loves to brag. She couldn't keep a secret to save her life."

The shaking slowly subsided, but in its place crept a cold absence. A hollow void. What if Lora was right? "He wouldn't do that," I whispered so softly I wasn't sure she could hear me.

Goosebumps rose along my arms. A frigid finger deliberately grazed down my spine. I recoiled, knowing exactly what the sensation meant.

"Stop that!" I screamed to the ceiling, throwing my arms out at my side. My fingernails dug into the tender flesh of my palm, trying to feel something other than the chill Doug's presence brought. The fact that it was Doug didn't freak me so much as the fact that it was a ghost doing the touching. Sebastian wrapped an arm around my back. His warmth enveloped me, thawing the arctic tingles running along my back. "Let's go outside and talk."

The mania subsided with the safety of his embrace, and he guided me out the front door. As we settled on the top step, Lora came running out, flapping her hands.

"Oh, fuck no. You aren't leaving me in there with *him*." She ran past us and stood on the walkway. "What are we doing, people? Are we exorcising a demon or are we just gonna stand around on the porch?" She looked Sebastian up and down. "Time to get rid of a ghost, pretty boy."

"Pretty boy?" Sebastian choked on a laugh. "Why is everybody calling me a *boy* today?" He looked skyward, probably for divine intervention, and shook his head.

Lora didn't respond, just crossed her arms and stared.

The sun peeked out from behind the clouds, blinding me in the process. I blinked and followed the sound of birds chirping from a nearby tree. Everything outside appeared normal. Too normal. How could everyday life just keep moving forward when, inside my house, a ghost terrorized my very existence and threatened my sanity?

The million dollar question? How was I supposed to move on with my life when my dead fiancé wouldn't move on with his death?

My chin dropped to my chest. I stared between my bent knees and asked sullenly, "Did Doug really talk Valerie into having my party at her house?"

"Yes," Lora answered, joining me on the steps. "I didn't want to tell you. I wanted you to have this happy image of your fiancé. And when he was alive, you *were* happy." She patted my knee and then rested her hand there, offering me the comfort I so desperately needed. "You never saw how controlling he was with you. How he'd manipulate things to keep you where he wanted."

I smiled weakly at Sebastian and Lora on either side of me, then turned to stare out past the road. I focused on nothing; the tall, proud structures lining the other side of the street faded away while I got lost in thought. "He used to pop up at the office to have lunch with me. I never thought anything of it, but looking back, he was checking up on my boss. I wondered why he'd always ask about him."

Lora slid her hand from my knee, but wrapped that arm around my back, pulling me snug to her side. "You told me the other day he sometimes helped pick out your clothes for the day."

"Yeah, he did. He had some pretty good fashion sense." I rested my head on her shoulder.

She leaned her head against mine. "No, sweetie, he was making sure you didn't wear anything he didn't approve of. I told you, he was a douche."

I sat up straight, bumping heads with Lora. I mentally catalogued the times he'd stepped in to help me pick out my clothes. "Oh, my God. You're right! If I'd picked out a top showing off my shoulders or too much belly, he'd tell me all the reasons it wouldn't work with the bottoms I'd chosen. One time, he'd said my legs were too white to show off that much skin. He'd made me put back that flowery skirt you bought me for my birthday."

"I tried to tell you," Lora chided.

She had. She was absolutely right. All those veiled questions she'd asked me to get me to realize how Doug had me under his thumb. The signs were all there, but I'd refused to see them, until now. He'd been a control freak.

"Oh my God," I breathed out. "That bastard!" Dry eyes greeted me for the first time. My tear ducts were empty. I was done crying for a man who couldn't take my feelings into consideration. I wouldn't let another tear fall for someone who needed to be in control of every minute of my life, even in his afterlife.

"That's the spirit!" She patted me on the back and

jumped up, slamming her fists onto her hips. "What's the plan?"

Sebastian stood as well, and I instantly felt the absence of him. "The plan is, I have an appointment I need to get to." He glanced at his phone to check the time. "I really wish I didn't."

Lora arched an eyebrow. "Is this a mystical appointment or a Magic Mike appointment?"

"It doesn't matter." I rose from the step, putting myself between the two. "Sebastian has a job that he needs to do. We'll figure out something until he can return."

"I've got three appointments scheduled today. If the third one doesn't run over, I'll see about coming back tonight and figuring out how we can get Doug to move on."

"In the meantime, Lora and I will go grab a bite to eat since her fat shoes smashed our lunch." I glanced behind me at my front door. Did I have enough nerve left in me to go get my things? "Uh, do I have to go back in there to get my purse?"

"Girl, leave it. My purse is in the car, and my keys are in my pocket." Lora chuckled. "You don't even need to lock the door. I'm sure Doug will keep the thieves out."

II

I lounged alone on the concrete steps in front of my porch, scared to high heaven to go inside and face my worst nightmare. The memory of Doug's icy touch traveling down my spine set my nerves on edge.

The battery life on my phone flashed fifteen percent and let out a pitiful beep, letting me know death would soon follow if I didn't plug it into a charger. Death appeared to be the running theme for me this week. I seriously needed to jot down some better ideas for next week to liven things up.

The problem was, my charger rested snugly inside my house in the drawer of my nightstand. The nightstand which currently resided in my haunted bedroom.

When Lora had abandoned me twenty minutes ago, an apology on her lips and a big hug just for me, my heart had sank into my stomach. She had work in the morning and not enough sick days to help me with my brand of crazy afterlife issues.

I, on the other hand, still had a couple days left of my

bereavement period. Work gave me a whole week to mourn the loss of Doug. A week seemed so insignificant. Who could get their shit together in a week after having a loved one ripped brutally from their life?

My phone beeped out another dismal whine. "I know, I know! Ugh!"

Sebastian had better answer my text soon. Preferably before my phone kicked the bucket. I wasn't brave enough to go in the house by myself. Not without Lora. Not without Sebastian. And definitely not with ghost Doug flying around with his jackass self as he knocked stuff over.

Then a thought popped up. Maybe I had it all wrong. Maybe Doug was just a clumsy ghost. Maybe? Naw. I shook that crazy thought from my head. No, Doug was a controlling asshole, plain and simple.

I heaved myself off the step and whirled around to face the house. Mustering up an ounce of courage, even to get my car keys, felt like the weight of the world pressing down on me.

If Sebastian didn't show up soon, I'd need to stay at a friend's house or a hotel. *Shit. Scratch that.* I'd just have to stay at a friend's. I had no means to pay for transportation to get there with my stuff trapped inside.

My mom would be the first person I'd call if I had more charge on my phone. I couldn't call and talk to Valerie or Helen. I'd made Lora swear she wouldn't say anything to either one of them about the activities happening here. Especially Valerie.

A chime rang out and a text message flashed across my screen: *Be there in ten minutes.*

My shoulders sagged in relief. Sebastian would be here soon. He'd help me to get rid of Doug's ghost and send him to rest in peace. Yet, even as I felt better that he'd be here, my anxiety kicked up a notch.

We'd be alone without Lora buffer between us.

Sebastian had made it clear he was interested in me from the beginning. I climbed the steps and paced back and forth on the porch, arms crossed. He'd also seemed ashamed about hitting on me after finding out about Doug's death. Would he still be interested or would he want to give me space instead? Funny, I'd always waited months before starting a new relationship in the past, but this felt different. This felt like it could truly be real and that scared the shit out of me. It scared me more than the ghost inside my house. Maybe the idea of marrying Doug hadn't scared me as much because it didn't truly feel real. Had I given my whole heart to Doug by the time he asked for my hand in marriage? I couldn't honestly answer. So many things had marred the image I had of him in my mind.

While I tried to straighten out the thoughts in my head, Sebastian pulled into the driveway.

Relief washed over me like a relaxing, hot shower. A dull ache settled into the muscles of my neck and shoulders from the tension and worry of waiting.

He walked with the same purposeful gait he had the first night he'd come up the walkway to my house. A white plastic bag dangled in his right hand, and he shouldered another bag on his left side. The smell of Chinese food hit me and my mouth watered.

"You brought food?" I questioned. "I thought we were going to get rid of a ghost, not—"

"Go on a date?" he finished.

"Exactly, because, you know—" I trailed off, not knowing how to finish that statement.

He grinned. "I know."

"Did you bring a laptop?" I asked, fidgeting nervously with my cuticles. It'd been a few years since I'd been a part of the dating scene, and even then, I wouldn't have considered myself an expert at it. I folded my hands in front of me to keep from tearing up my skin.

Most of the guys that found me attractive were not as hot as Sebastian. I felt way out of my element.

"I did. I need it to do some research on how to get rid of Doug." He handed me the bag of Chinese. "Where would you like to eat dinner?"

"Let's take this around back. There's a swing back there we can sit on." I guided him to the back side of the porch. "What would you have done if I'd hated Chinese?"

He propped his laptop bag against the side of the house and eased down onto the swing. "I would've looked like an ass, but then went and got you something else."

Peeking inside the bag, I found egg rolls, fortune cookies, and containers that appeared to contain chicken fried rice and other assorted meats. "I call dibs on picking the first fortune cookie!"

Sebastian chuckled. "Deal."

He held the swing still for me while I sat down next to him. He scooted closer, his thigh flush and warm against my own. A different kind of warmth radiated throughout the rest of my body. I hoped the porch light didn't give away my blush if I had one.

I avoided looking up at him, afraid of what I might see in those blue eyes of his. Instead, I started taking out containers and setting them in his lap and on the other side of me.

"Ahh! That's hot!" He moved one box of food over to sit beside him on the swing.

I winced. "Sorry." Rummaging around in the bag, I pulled out two sets of paper-wrapped sticks. "I'm also sorry to tell you chopsticks will be your choice of utensil tonight. I'm not going inside that house to get you a fork."

He shrugged. "Okay. I know how to use them, do you?"

A sheepish smile spread across my face. "I'm sorta, kinda okay... *ish* at using chopsticks."

"Is that so? It's not so bad. You'll get the hang of them." He grabbed a pair. "Here, let me show you how it's done."

Sebastian pulled out the two sticks from the paper. "See? You place the first chopstick in the crook of your hand while using your thumb to press it down onto your ring finger to stabilize it. The second chopstick goes on top of that and you use your middle and index finger to open and close it." He demonstrated how the top stick moved to open and close at the end so you could pick up food. "Easy, right?"

"You make it look easy, but I have a feeling I'm going to starve tonight."

The delicious smell of chicken fried rice intensified when he popped open one of the cardboard containers. "I wouldn't let you starve. I'll feed you myself if I have to."

I swallowed. Hard. I was bombarded with images of him feeding me, the chopsticks sliding excruciatingly slow between my lips. Maybe his eyes would wander over the contours of my face, landing on my lips, and he'd think about kissing me?

Heat flushed my face, and I turned away to survey the backyard. Crickets chirped from a nearby bush. The moon, hanging fat in the sky, peered down at me through the tree branches surrounding the porch. It appeared to be almost full. Just a few more days. I loved that my new yard was boxed in by beautiful brick walls. They were so much nicer than a traditional fence.

"Can you pass the orange chicken?" He took another bite, but pointed with his chopsticks to the container beside me, clearly labeled on top.

"Oh!" I jerked in my seat like I'd be caught with my hand in the cookie jar. "Yeah, sure." I popped open the top and practically drooled at the smell.

Unwrapping my own set of chopsticks, I poked one of the sticks into a piece of orange chicken and then handed the container to Sebastian.

He gasped. "I thought I taught you better. Barbarian!"

"Hey, this barbarian is hungry." I shoved the chicken into my mouth and silently threatened him with my newly acquired weapons.

Sebastian set his boxes to the side, pulled out his laptop, and fired it up. He called up a search engine and got to business.

I made room for myself as well and curled my legs up on the swing while I leaned into his shoulder. With a box of fried rice topped by orange chicken, I did my best to shovel food into my mouth and watch him.

"Any good hits?" I let out a squeak as rice toppled from my chopsticks and landed in his lap. "Oops."

He smashed his lips together and tried not to laugh. "I've got a few ideas. Most of my clients only want me to contact the dead. I've only tried to help a ghost pass on once since I started this business." He typed in a new search phrase and browsed the links. "This isn't a one size fits all kind of deal. Some ghosts are more stubborn than others. And with the backlash we've gotten from Doug, I want to be sure I have a dozen tricks up my sleeves."

I finished chewing and set the box down in my lap to lean closer to his screen. "Do you think—"

The question fell short when Sebastian turned. His lips were centimeters from my own. I sucked in a breath and held it, unsure of whether to cross this line or not.

Sebastian looked just as conflicted as I felt. His breathing picked up, his eyes searching mine, asking or seeking permission.

My face must have given him the answer he needed.

His warm, soft lips pressed to mine. Tingles of excitement spread from the contact, lighting up my world behind my eyelids. My body melted into his as his arms wrapped around me and pulled me close.

Suddenly, Sebastian jumped back, and I wondered if I'd done something wrong. Was I a bad kisser?

His hands snatched at his laptop, barely catching it as it slid from his lap. "Shit," he muttered, closing it quickly. He set it down on the porch, then turned to me, mischief gleaming in his eyes. "Now where were we?"

Before I could reply, his lips smashed into mine, searing

me all the way down to my soul. Strong arms wrapped around me and pulled me flush with his side. I'd felt the muscles of his arms before, but never wrapped around my body like this. I melted into him.

When I felt the box of fried rice and chicken hit the porch, I chose to ignore it. I'd clean it up later. Right now, I had more important things taking up my attention.

Suddenly, a loud pop rang out, and the tinkle of broken glass falling to the porch interrupted the mood.

We broke our kiss. I held back a scream of surprise as I pressed a hand to my heart. "What the fuck was that?"

Sebastian pushed off the swing and went to investigate. "Looks like the porch light burst."

"Why would it just break like that? Unless..."

"It appears things have gotten worse." He held out his arm to keep me from stepping on the glass. "Be careful."

Careful was the furthest thought from my mind. I was done with being careful. If Doug could squeeze his presence outside of this house and have enough influence to affect the lightbulb, what else could he do?

It was time to be ruthless.

I2

anic set in as I awoke to a strange, dark room. I
patted down the bed and looked around to see if I'd
be making the walk of shame or not, but the room-
darkening curtains blocked off any chance of figuring that
out. Then reality caught up with me. Last night, after the
light bulb incident, Sebastian didn't think it was safe for me
to sleep in my own house. He'd offered me his guest
bedroom.

My phone lay on the oak nightstand, fully charged. I sat
up in bed and used the flashlight to look around. Definitely
alone. Sebastian had been the perfect gentleman last night.
Why did he have to be so damn nice? After that searing kiss
last night, I'd wanted anything but a gentlemanly attitude
from him.

I unplugged my phone and skimmed through the
notifications. One of them was a text from my mother asking
how I was doing. In all of this, I'd never called her like she'd

asked me to. At the funeral, she'd been adamant I call her to talk.

Maybe my mom could help me sort out my feelings. I pulled up her contact, hit call, and pressed the phone to my ear.

"Hey, sweetie. How are you this morning?" she asked, her voice soothing.

"I'm good, Mom. As best as can be expected." Telling my mom about my ghost problem was out of the question, but I could test the waters and see what she thought about Sebastian. Would she think I was rushing things?

"That's all anyone could ask during a time like this. Have you eaten? Do I need to bring you breakfast? How about I head over and bring you some coffee and one of those struesels you love from Ann's Bakery?"

Her litany of questions ran through my head on loop, and I tried to figure out which one to answer first. "Is this twenty questions?"

"I just want to make sure you're taking care of yourself. You're my baby!"

"I know, but I'm not at home right now." I figured I'd slowly slide this new development into the conversation.

"Are you over at Valerie's or Lora's?" She knew Helen didn't have the space for me with a husband and kids. It was believable that I could be at either of the other's two houses to not feel so alone.

"No, I'm not at either of their houses." I bit my lip. "I met a guy."

"Oh, my God, Josie. It's not even been a week, and you're already shacked up with another guy?" She scoffed, and I could feel her judgement radiating through the phone. This conversation was not going as planned.

Shaking my head at her rant, I strengthened my resolve. She would not bully me about this. I thought my mother, of all people, would understand. She'd always told me I could talk to her about anything and everything. Guess not. "I'm not shacked up with him. I slept in his guest bedroom last night. He was very nice and didn't make any passes at me. He… didn't want me to be alone all by myself in that big house."

The door creaked open and Sebastian popped his head into the room. "Breakfast?"

I answered him with a smile and a nod, pointing to the phone and mouthing "Mom."

He gave me a thumbs up and closed the door behind him. "Was that him?"

"Yes, Mom." I sighed. "You'll be happy to know he's making breakfast. I won't wither away to nothing."

"I'm sorry. I… you just caught me off guard. Is he a nice Christian boy?"

There was that word again. Boy. He definitely was *not* a boy.

"And if he isn't?" I shot back.

"Now you're just messing with me." I could picture her pressing her fingers to the bridge of her nose like she did when she stressed about something. "You're a smart girl. I know your emotions are all over the place. Just… be careful."

Careful. That word was beginning to drive me crazy.

"Don't worry. I will." I lied. I planned quite the opposite.

I'd been careful my whole life. When did I get to become reckless and abandon caution to the wind?

Her voice pepped up some when she asked, "So where did you meet him?"

Shit. How did I explain? *Mom, I met him the first time as he took off the majority of his clothes for my bachelorette party. And the second time I met him, he came to my house to help exorcise a ghost from it. The ghost of my dead fiancé, to be exact.*

"Um, just while I was out with Lora one day." I hesitated, trying to formulate a believable story. "Lora had come over to make sure I didn't stay cooped up in the house unpacking boxes."

"Aww, she's such a good friend to you," she cooed. "Where did you two go?"

She wasn't going to let up on this.

"We, um, we went to that new club that just opened up across town." I hadn't actually been yet, but I racked my brain for the information I'd read about the new establishment. "It's a club for women to let loose and have fun. They screen the guys before letting them in. So, if Sebastian was able to get in, then he must be okay."

"Sebastian? That's a lovely name. Very wholesome."

I rolled my eyes. Only my mom would consider a name *wholesome.*

"Listen, I probably need to get downstairs before breakfast is done."

"I agree. You need to eat and keep your strength up. Losing Doug may have crushed you and left you lonely, but honestly, I'm glad that you've found someone to make you smile."

"Me too, Mom," I spoke wistfully. "Me too."

"Go eat your breakfast and call me this weekend."

"Will do."

I rolled out of bed, feeling more refreshed than I had all week. A good night's sleep did my body good. Shoving my cell phone into my back pocket, I stretched my arms above my head.

Sebastian's face peeked through the door, his eyes trailing a heat-filled gaze down my body and stopping on the exposed skin of my belly. My shirt had lifted up while I stretched.

My arms dropped, and I adjusted my shirt, flushed. "Is... is breakfast ready?"

He winked and opened the door wide. "It sure is." His fingers laced with mine and he tugged me along through his modern house. His home was recently built in a new development. Soft, neutral tones covered the walls, while striking bold colors accented in little splashes here and there. I'd wondered last night if he'd hired an interior decorator or if he had a natural affinity for design.

Seated at his breakfast nook, I admired the way his body moved. He was a work of art as he carried plates of food over to the table and set them down in front of me.

I knew a way to a man's heart was through his stomach, but how had this role reversed? He'd brought me food last night and now, here he was, *cooking* me breakfast. Was there nothing this man couldn't do?

"This looks delicious." Fork in hand, I started on the eggs. They were light and fluffy. Next, I slathered a dollop of butter onto the pancakes from a tub on the table.

Sebastian set his own plates down and then slid the syrup my way.

If my pancakes could talk, they'd scream for mercy as I drowned them in syrup. I cut a slice of pancake out, cut a piece off my sausage, then stabbed both and devoured them. I loved pancakes and sausage.

"Did Lora call to check up on you?" Sebastian inquired.

"No, I called my mom." I took another bite of eggs, chewed, and swallowed. "She'd told me to keep in touch with her after... last weekend. I figured I'd call and let her know I was still alive."

"Did you tell her about the ghost?" He took a sip of his coffee, eyeing me over the rim.

I snorted. "No. She wouldn't have believed me. I'd have been put into a mental hospital before I could even scream ghost." I poured in some cream into the coffee cup waiting for me. Spooning in sugar, I stirred until it turned a light brown. "She asked me if you were a good Christian boy."

He nearly spit his coffee out. "What? So you two had a conversation about *me*?"

"Yeah." I took a savoring sip of my own coffee, closing my eyes as it worked its magic. "I might have mentioned you once."

"Okay, I deserved that." He set his mug down. "What did you tell her?"

"Huh?"

"When she asked if I was a good Christian boy, did you answer her?" His lips turned down and he pivoted in his chair so his body faced me.

"Are you?"

"No."

I let a half-smile slip out as I gazed at him. I thought at first he was mad at me, but after a second examination, I realized he was worried. Worried I'd reject him because of his beliefs perhaps?

"What about you?" he asked.

"Well," I swallowed. "It's complicated." And it was. I hadn't been to church in quite some time. Mainly, because Doug had decided for me. Now, I wasn't sure what to make of my beliefs.

Especially now that I knew ghosts were real.

13

"Religion usually is. Complicated that is." His fork scraped the plate as he pushed his eggs around. He was back to being worried again.

"You don't have to worry." I reached out and gripped his wrist to still his nervous motions. "I don't care what religion you are."

"That's not it. I want to apologize about last night," he said into his pancakes.

"Apologize? About what?"

"For kissing you. I shouldn't have." His gaze darted over the table, still refusing to meet mine. "I should have respected you enough to let you grieve. You just lost someone close to you. I... I'm an ass."

I squeezed his wrist. "Don't apologize."

Blue eyes lifted to connect with mine. Sebastian's eyebrows met in the middle in a pained expression, one that broke my heart. "I just don't want to mess this up."

"You won't." I gave one final squeeze and brought my hand to my lap.

He shook his head. "I don't think you understand. In all my years on this earth, in all the time I've spent with both the living and the dead, I've never felt a connection like I have with you. I felt that first spark the night of your party and I haven't been able to stop thinking about you. What if it was fate that planted me on your doorstep to look for a ghost?"

My throat pinched shut. "I... Sebastian."

"See? I've already fucked it up." His fork clattered to his plate, and his chin dropped to his chest on a deep exhale.

Pushing my chair back, I stood from the table. Sebastian's shoulders became rigid. "You haven't fucked anything up." I slid his plate back, then threw a leg over his chair, settling down in his lap facing him. The strong, confident man I'd witnessed strutting up my sidewalk returned.

His pupils dilated as he lifted his head, and we locked gazes.

My lips brushed against the shell of his ear, whispering, "I feel it, too."

Strong hands gripped my hips, and Sebastian let out a deep growl.

This time, I initiated the kiss. Sebastian hadn't done anything he needed to apologize for last night, and I needed to show him that. I would tell him without words that any slight imagined was forgiven.

His lips slanted over mine, deepening the kiss, and I

opened my mouth in invitation. I gripped the sides of his face and kissed him like I planned to devour him.

Breakfast long forgotten, I moved my hips against his, cursing the fabric that separated us when I felt the evidence of his arousal.

"You've got to stop that, Josie."

I nipped at his bottom lip, grinning. "No, I don't."

"You do if you want me to keep your virtue intact."

A laugh escaped before I could control myself. "My virtue hasn't been intact in quite some time, Sebastian."

"Happiness suits you." He wrapped an arm around my torso and yanked me forward, my chest now flush with his. "Tell me to stop."

"Don't stop," I teased.

"Are you sure?" His arm around me trembled. He could barely contain himself.

I worried my bottom lip between my teeth coyly and nodded. "I want this."

The chair clattered to the floor behind him, and I was suddenly airborne. He threw me over his shoulder, his arm securing my legs. My blonde hair swayed back and forth as I saw stairs passing by below me.

"Sebastian!" I screamed, smacking his ass. "Put me down."

"Oh, I'll put you down alright." He shouldered the door open, and I got my first glimpse of his bedroom before my world blurred by and I landed on his bed.

"Eek!" I managed to squeak out before Sebastian's body covered mine. We were both still fully clothed and to me, that was just too much between us. I wanted - no *needed* - to feel his skin against mine. I needed something good to happen in my life. Something of my choosing, not something someone else dictated for me.

This was me throwing caution to the wind and following my heart. *Careful* no longer had a place in my vocabulary list.

His lips trailed soft kisses over my neck and shoulder. He tugged my shirt down, then growled in frustration.

Wiggling beneath him, I brought my arms to the hem of my shirt and tried to raise it up.

"No." He halted my progress. "I want to do this right."

"I have no doubt in my mind you're doing this right," I panted out. "I just—"

His hand glided under my shirt, brushing skin against skin, effectively shutting me up. He cupped my breast through the bra and swallowed loud enough for me to hear." If we do this too fast, it'll be over soon. Just," he breathed in slowly and then let it out. "Let's make it last."

"Okay." I released my grip on the hem and let him explore beneath my shirt. He bit playfully through my top at my breast, and I sucked in a gasp.

"Damnit," he grumbled to himself. His fingers fumbled for the edge of my shirt and in one smooth motion had it up and over my head. "You're killing my self control here."

I tugged on his shirt. "Then stop holding back."

He tore his shirt over his head and threw it to join mine on the floor. While he worked at his belt and jeans, I unhooked my bra and tossed it aside. I'd always been self conscious of my body, but having Sebastian pause, dumbfounded, to rake his gaze down the front of me, I no longer felt lacking.

Everything in his gaze made me feel gorgeous and wanted. The rest of our clothes were quickly discarded and in seconds Sebastian was back to worshipping my body.

His mouth traveled a path downward with kisses, nips, and licks. Each touch sending a shiver down my body. His lips reached the apex of my thighs, and I held my breath, waiting. He spread my legs wider and kissed the inside of my thighs. Everywhere but where I'd expected him to. Each kiss and lick edged closer, heightening my anticipation.

When two of his fingers slid inside, I released the breath I'd held on a shudder. I cried out when he sucked my clit into his mouth.

"Sebastian, what are you doing to me?"

"Hmmmm?" he asked, sending vibrations through those thousands of nerve endings.

My hands gripped the sheets as his tongue drew circles around the bud and his fingers worked their way in and out of me slowly. He withdrew his hand, then added a third finger, picking up his pace. In and out his fingers slid. Faster and faster. He teeth nipped at my sensitive skin, then sucked it in even harder.

My eyes clenched shut, and I arched my back as stars flashed across my vision. My orgasm washed over me like a tidal wave, carrying me away, and leaving me adrift.

When I finally came back down to earth, Sebastian was ripping open a foil square with his teeth. He rolled the condom down his length and settled himself between my thighs.

"Last chance."

"What?" Color me confused.

"To back out."

"Oh, fuck no." I thrust my hips to meet his, feeling the tip graze my folds. It'd been a month since I'd had sex. Something else that had been withheld from me in the name of control. Something about waiting so we could make our wedding night special. I'd thought it sweet at the time.

I scrubbed thoughts of my ex from my mind and focused on the intent look on Sebastian's face.

He rolled his hips and slid inside, the fullness surprising me.

A moan escaped me as I pressed my hips into his.

His lips set into a thin line as he pumped in and out of me slowly, his arms shaking as he held himself up.

"Let go, Sebastian." I hooked my ankles behind him and met him thrust for thrust.

He shook his head, sweat beading on his forehead. "I won't last if I do."

"I've already had mine." I ran my nails along his back, not expecting a reaction. He closed his eyes and groaned. "Did you like that?"

"Please, don't do that again." His control only held on by a thread.

I dragged my nails down his skin once again and that thread snapped.

He slid out of me and rose up on his knees, breaking my ankles apart. In one quick motion, he'd flipped me over and drove back into me from behind, pumping furiously. His fingers dug into the flesh around my hips as he moaned. I'd poked the beast, but I regretted nothing.

The pleasure built back up at an alarming rate as skin

smacked against skin. The sound only spiked my pleasure, sending me over the edge again. I cried out with my cheek pressed to the sheets and my fingers digging into the mattress.

Sebastian slammed into me one last time, grunting. His body jerked as he rode out his release.

I collapsed onto the bed, my body spent and sated. He fell down next to me and pulled my back to his chest while he caught his breath.

The theme of the week no longer needed to be changed, because right now, I'd died and gone to heaven.

14

The house looked creepier from the sidewalk than it had the first time I laid eyes on it. When I first toured it during the open house, I'd been enamored with the architecture and vintage feel. Knowledge was a powerful thing, and right now, it powered my imagination, knowing Doug still floated around inside doing ghosty things. What other chaos awaited me once I walked through those doors?

"You could always try to sell it and move again," Sebastian offered.

"No." I stood rooted to the sidewalk. "Would you want to subject anyone else to him?"

"You're right, but it was worth a shot." He looked to the street. "Lora and Helen are here."

Lora knew the story, but I wondered what she'd had to do to convince Helen to tag along for this adventure.

"Good. This needs to end, and it ends today." I crossed my arms, a chill alighting my skin that had nothing to do with the weather. I knew it wasn't Doug; it was my nerves. My stomach churned at the thought of facing my dead fiancé. How much would he fight us?

"Hey, girl," Helen said as she approached. "You doing alright?"

"I'll be doing better once this is over." I uncrossed my arms and walked up the path. Sebastian caught up with me and laced his fingers with mine.

We filed into the house and headed toward the dining room. There, we surrounded the circular table and started setting up for the seance.

Sebastian spread out a black tablecloth before pulling things from a canvas tote. Candles ran in a circle toward the center of the table, only a few inches apart from each other. We each took turns with the lighter and lit the candle in front of us.

"What next?" I asked, handing Sebastian back his lighter.

Reaching into his great big bag of everything, he pulled out a crystal ball. A for real, genuine crystal ball complete with a little wooden holder.

"Does that thing really work?" Helen asked.

"It does. I use it for crystal ball divination. Sometimes it helps me see things clearer." He gingerly set it in the middle of the circle of candles. "Everyone take a seat."

We each picked a wooden chair and settled into it. I had Sebastian on my right and Lora on my left. Across from me Helen sat, wide eyed with wonder.

"Everyone, reach out and hold the hand of the person on either side of you. This creates a circle and a sacred place." He reached out for my hand first, giving it a reassuring squeeze.

We all connected through our hands, sharing the same nervous energy.

"Doug," Sebastian started out. "We ask you to enter this circle. Come forth and show your presence."

The room remained silent. The only sounds were the creaking and settling of the house. Helen sniffed and I gave her a sharp look. She rolled her eyes and looked around the table.

"Spirit in this house, we ask that you come to us," Sebastian tried.

Helen cleared her throat and gave a pointed look to Sebastian. "Is this shit even real. Are you real?"

"Shh," he hushed her. "We don't need negative energy in our circle."

Lora pursed her lips and stared at Helen, trying to convey without words for her to shut the fuck up. Three, that made three times I'd witnessed Lora being quiet when required. She was on a roll. If she kept it up, maybe there was a place for her in the *Guiness Book of World Records*.

Sebastian tried again. "Doug, if you're still in this house, give us a sign."

"Do you think maybe he left on his own?" Hope filled my chest to bursting. Wouldn't it be wonderful if he'd left of his own accord and I could get on with my life?

A gust of wind swirled around the room. Helen's hair flipped over into her face, the tablecloth fluttered at the ends, and half the candles went out.

Helen screamed and shook the hair out of her face, but Sebastian and Lora held her hands in a firm grip, refusing to let go.

"Don't break the circle, Helen," Lora whispered over the howl of another gust of wind.

"Seems good ol' Doug is still here with us." Sebastian looked into the crystal ball. The remaining candle flames flickered on its reflective surface. He spoke up over the chaos in the room. "Doug, this is no longer your house. It's time for you to move on and leave this place. We wish you well in your spiritual journey."

Did we really? But I quickly shut that thought down. We didn't need negative thoughts either. If Doug wouldn't leave, I was scared what measures Sebastian would need to take. He'd told me some of the information he'd found. Some good, some bad.

The bad concerned me the most. Depending on how stubborn Doug the douche wanted to be, we might be getting into some tricky spellwork, he said.

Helen jerked against her bonds. "I'm done. I don't want to do this anymore!" Her eyes had widened to the size of dinner plates.

"Deep breath. It's just a little wind. Sebastian has it under control." Lora nodded to him. "Right?"

"Right." But he didn't sound convincing. Sebastian was used to contacting the dead and chit-chatting, not telling them to go take a hike. Big difference. He went on. "Everybody, keep your hands together, but stand up."

As one, we pushed our chairs back with our legs and then stood.

"Doug Branton. I order you to leave this place now!" Sebastian called out loudly, his words echoing throughout the half empty house.

The wind died down to a breeze, but the flames of the candles still flickered wildly. Doug was putting up quite a fight. Something shattered in the kitchen, and I cringed, hoping it wasn't any of my grandmother's china.

Sebastian leaned to look into the doorway of the kitchen. "Doug, whatever is holding you here to this plane or whatever you feel you need to do here, it's no longer important. You need to move on!"

Doug's spirit flashed in and out of view near the ceiling right in the middle of our circle.

Helen's face drained of all color.

"Helen. HELEN! Do not pass out!" I screamed across the table.

"We need to try the spell." Sebastian's face gleamed with sweat and not in the way I wanted it to.

He closed his eyes and dipped his head.

Ashes to ashes, dust to dust.
Unwanted spirit, leave you must.
Move on from this plane, pack up and leave.
Hold on no more, and let us grieve.

The wind stopped abruptly, and the candle flames stopped flickering. Had it worked? Maybe we should've tried the spell to begin with.

"The wind stopped," Lora stated the obvious.

"Oh. My God," Helen punctuated her words. "What the fuck was all that?"

The room began to spin, and the candlelight dimmed.

"Sebastian, I don't feel so well." I swayed and nearly face-planted into the table.

Without thinking, Sebastian reached out and caught me.

My consciousness felt shoved to the back, and I no longer had control of my body. I tried to move a hand or blink an eye, but nothing happened.

Sebastian! I'm in here! I tried to scream, but I only heard the words in my head.

"I won't give her up so easily," I heard my voice say from far away, but the words weren't mine. *Where did my words go?* I kept trying to move my mouth, to make my vocal cords work, to get some signal to my friends that I was still in here, but to no avail.

Nerves in my skin still sent signals of touch and pain, though. My knuckles burned for some reason.

"You asshole," Sebastian yelled through a tunnel. Scuffling sounds filtered to the dark void I floated in, and my body ached in places it shouldn't. The darkness disoriented me, and I had no clue what was going on around me. Did I pass out or was this all a dream?

The dizziness overwhelmed me to the point I felt sick to my stomach. My body lurched back, my control still gone, and I fell... down, down, down while a soft chanting of words whispered across my mind, until the blackness swallowed me whole.

15

"She's waking up!" someone shouted too close to my ear.

Footsteps pounded against the hardwood floor, enhancing the pain radiating in my head.

"Shh, don't startle her. She's been through an ordeal."

The second voice belonged to Sebastian.

Pressed against the hardwood floor, my back ached, and my head pounded out a rhythm I would have been impressed with had it not equaled pain. My eyes fluttered open slowly, and I found three pairs of concerned eyes staring down at me.

Helen still hadn't regained any color, but at least she hadn't passed out like me.

"What happened?" I moaned. Hair tickled my neck and I brushed it away, then felt around my scalp for any injuries.

Sebastian ignored my question. "How are you feeling?"

"Like I got hit and run over by a Mack truck and then it decided to back up to finish the job."

JENNIFER LASLIE

Lora laid a wet rag over my forehead. The coolness soothed the ache, and I was thankful for even the slightest relief.

"Can I sit up now?" This floor wasn't the most comfortable place to rest. The ache in my back hadn't been near as bad as the time I'd slept on the couch.

Sebastian put a hand under my head. "Yes, but not too fast." He assisted me in sitting up and then put an arm under my legs and behind my back, hoisting me into the air. He carried me to the living room and eased me onto a couch cushion.

"Better?" He held my stare for a moment, then proceeded to check me over.

"Much, but you didn't tell me what happened."

He ignored me, continuing his ministrations. "You're not bleeding anywhere."

Helen staggered into the room in a daze. She wobbled to the other side of the couch and plopped down. "I don't know if I'll ever look at the world the same now." Her eyes stared off into the distance, and I wondered if we'd scarred my friend for life. Did Austin have a therapist who specialized in ghost trama?

Sebastian and Lora exchanged glances. Lora nodded to Sebastian, and they both sighed simultaneously.

"I don't like being in the dark here." I really didn't. Whatever had gone on inside my head better not be something I repeated, ever. "Did I pass out?"

"Sorta," Lora said, shrugging her shoulders.

"Doug didn't want to leave without a fight. He possessed you and tried to attack me." Sebastian grabbed the hand that didn't hurt and held it tight.

"That would explain why my knuckles hurt." I gasped. "Did I hurt you?"

Sebastian turned his head to show the other side of his face. He had a nice-sized bruise blooming by his ear. "He swung and I tried to dodge him, but he still managed to connect, even with your tiny hands."

"I'm so sorry!" I reached up to inspect it, but then hesitated. "It's already turning purple."

"This wasn't your fault at all, Josie. Please don't blame yourself. Doug is the one who took over your body. He controlled your movements, not you."

"Douche," Lora whispered.

Sebastian snorted. "Well, Doug the douche is officially gone."

"How did you manage to get him to leave?" I asked. Doug's stubbornness had kept him in this house for longer than I'd liked.

"Remember the spell I tried?" He glanced at Lora and Helen, tipping his head at the two of them. "They both helped me chant it over and over until Doug was expelled from your body and forced to move on."

My head fell back against the couch. "Thank fucking God. He's gone."

Lora patted my leg, and I cringed from the pain, hissing out a breath.

"Sorry." She yanked her hand back. "I think it best if I take Helen home and give you some time to recover. If you need me, give me a call."

"Thank you, Lora." I smiled. "Thank you for believing me

and being there when I needed you most."

"Girl, that's what best friends are for." She rose from the couch. "I'd hug you, but you might break in half."

"I might." I laughed, the muscles in my stomach bunched up and shot pain through my abdomen. "Ow, okay, it hurts to laugh."

"Come on, Helen." Lora helped her to stand and ushered her to the car.

With my two friends gone, the house seemed especially quiet and empty. No more icy chills sweeping down my spine. No loud crashes echoing from other rooms. Sebastian and I were truly alone now.

"I meant what I said earlier."

"What's that?"

"About this connection we have. I know we didn't exactly start out like a normal couple."

The laugh couldn't be helped. I held my side as it rang out. "No, no we didn't."

"I'd like to take you out on a date once you feel better." He propped a pillow behind my back and moved the ottoman so I could put my feet up. "How does that sound?"

"I think it sounds wonderful. And I think it sounds like I can finally move on with my life now that Doug has moved on in his death."

Continue the Unfortunate Spells series in book one, How to Spell Disaster

https://authorjlaslie.com/books/unfortunatespells/

Join my newsletter and receive a FREE ebook!
https://sendfox.com/lp/1r82ev

HOW TO MAKE AN
ADIOS MOTHERFUCKER

This drink is not for the faint of heart. If you have a low tolerance to alcohol, you might want to pretend you never saw this drink recipe or maybe cut the ingredients in half and not exceed more than one drink.

- 1 oz gin
- 1 oz light rum
- 1 oz tequila
- 1.5 oz Blue Curacao liqueur
- 2 oz sweet and sour mix
- 1 oz Sprite

Shake the alcohol then add the sprite on top! Drink up and be prepared to kiss your ass goodbye! I have a two drink limit on these.

BOTTOMS UP!

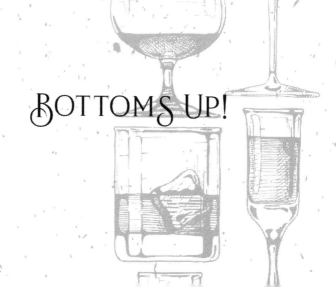

About the Author

Jennifer Laslie is a crazy cat lady who lives in Utah with her wonderful family. Her office affords her a mountain view that she loves! When she's not thinking about cheesecake or cats, she can be found in the bookstore in the Young Adult section, coffee in hand.

To learn more about Jennifer Laslie and the books she writes, visit authorjlaslie.com.

facebook.com/authorjlaslie

twitter.com/authorjlaslie

instagram.com/nytemirage

pinterest.com/nytemirage

bookbub.com/authors/jennifer-laslie

Acknowledgments

This book wouldn't be possible without the help of my husband. His brain comes up with some crazy ideas. When I'd come up with the titles for this series, I didn't have a story most of them. He threw a pitch for this title that had me questioning his sanity, but then the longer I thought about it, the more the idea kept growing and growing, until I knew I had to write it.

I also want to thank Heather Marie Adkins from Cyberwitch Press for editing this beauty and making her shine. She corrects my weirdo sentences and sets me straight. I don't know what I'd do without her.

Crystal Waldele, thank you for your proofreading and making sure the typos didn't slip through the cracks!

Thank you to all my author friends who encouraged me with writing sprints and laughed at the excerpts I sent them.

And last but not least, thank you to my early readers who reviewed this before it went live. Every message and review letting me know how much you loved it made my day! I hope both the early readers, and the ones just now getting a chance to put this book in their hands, enjoyed reading it as much as I enjoyed writing it.

Made in the USA
Las Vegas, NV
01 December 2021

35781356R00081